To Sarah

Please remember

I wrote this a

long time ago.

With love

Ricky Sedani

Summer 2009.

writer's block.

RICKY SEDANI

Printed in Victoria, Canada

National Library of Canada Cataloguing in Publication Data

Sedani, Ricky, 1983-
Writer's block / Ricky Sedani.

ISBN 1-55395-674-5

I. Title.

PR6119.E43W75 2003 823'.92 C2003-900582-8

TRAFFORD

Suite 6E, 2333 Government St., Victoria, B.C. V8T 4P4, CANADA
Phone 250-383-6864 Toll-free 1-888-232-4444 (Canada & US)
Fax 250-383-6804 E-mail sales@trafford.com
Web site www.trafford.com TRAFFORD PUBLISHING IS A DIVISION OF TRAFFORD HOLDINGS LTD.
Trafford Catalogue #03-0037 www.trafford.com/robots/03-0037.html

10 9 8 7 6 5 4 3 2

For Satish, Bina and Shaun.

prologue

I used to love Christmas. The excitement, the thrill, the food, the presents and the grandest fixation of them all, television. But things have changed in the new Millennium.

We are no longer young, the thrill has been passed down, the food makes us fat, the presents are now clothes and the most unpleasant of all the synonyms of the 25th December is that television has become boring. My generation is sick of watching the same films every year. We have become weary of the same 'Only Fools and Horses' Christmas specials and most of all, we are distraught to find that year after year nothing changes. We still watch 'The Jewel of the Nile,' and the Queen's speech and feel contented.

I could hear Emily crying in the distant background. The room seemed to grow colder. It was like there was a spiritual presence in the room, hovering over me. The doorbell rang. I ignored it; my head was comfortable resting on the arm of the sofa. The doorbell interrupted my deep concentration again.

'What?!' I yelled at the door hoping that whatever disturbance would disappear.

'Taxi,' the response meant that I had to move from my deeply comfortable position. I opened the door and sat back down.

'Vinny! Is that for me?' Her accent is what drew me to her in the first place. I remained quiet. I did not have the energy to speak. I sat waiting. Waiting. I was transfixed with the painting, which hung on the wall that we bought together. Cheesy yet artistic. The painting was in black and white. A little boy dressed as if he was going to a board meeting giving a rose to a little girl who looked like a child actor from the fifties. The rose was the only element of the picture that stood out. And then, suddenly, as if I had been woken up,

'I'll be out in a minute,' she ordered as the taxi driver already confined himself to his car and occupied himself with the car radio. She looked at me. She had these deep green eyes, soft, silky black hair and a smile that would break down any man onto his knees and cry. I hated that.

'What about the picture?' I questioned as if I was one of her students.

'Keep it,' she said this without even moving her lips. 'You knew this was going to happen. It can't be that much of a shock. Vinny, look at me, its better this way.' She paused. 'Emily!' She yelled.

I hated when Claire shouted at her. I lied; I hated the fact that she was not going to yell at me anymore. 'This is the last of my things. I'll call you when I get myself sorted and you can pick up Emily for the weekend. Emily entered the room in her Scooby Doo pyjamas that she insisted that I buy her.

She walked over to her mother. 'Go and give Daddy a big kiss.' Claire instructed her. I felt like crying. I couldn't. Emily looked at me as if it was I that was going away. I did not want my beautiful daughter to think that her old man was a wimp. And I did not want her to cry.

I held her close. My daughter. She is going to hate me in about twelve year's time but at this moment in time that consequence was of no importance. I promised her McDonalds at the weekend and after some deliberation, she ran back to her mother. Emily stood at the doorstep looking at the Taxi.

'I'm leaving. Call me before you pick Emily up. Is that okay?' She quietly uttered as she gathered her things.' I decided I was going to ignore her. There was a silence. 'Give me an answer! For Christ's sake! Stop being childish.' And then she left.

Without regret, without remorse, without looking back, she was gone. Both of them. I again rested my head against the arm of the sofa and curled my legs up. It was like in the movies. I felt like I was in a waiting room. The feeling of illness and boredom culminated in my stomach.

I looked around the empty house. The immense dark blue walls, the colossal and somewhat unnerving black and white framed pictures and my sofa. I am not a materialistic person but I believe it is a basic human right to have a sofa. I tried to sleep but could not. There were too many things going on in my head. I stared at the picture again. The reason the rose stood out was because it was the only object in the picture that was in colour. I named the rose Emily.

The cold wooden floor was covered with a thin light hand woven cream rug. Claire had an infatuation with things from Ikea. Or was it Habitat? I cannot remember. I do not care. I am now alone. By myself. After careful deliberation, I decided to reach over and get the remote. Television will numb my mind. I watched all the crap they usually show every Boxing Day.

It was not a white Christmas. It was a lonely, cold wet Christmas. Tinsel covered tree stood at the corner of the living room. I did not get the flashing lights because, well, they annoy me. Claire wanted a real tree. Subsequently, Emily wanted a chocolate tree. I spent my day off buying, decorating and marvelling at that tree. It was beautiful. I spent the afternoon watching Christmas special after Christmas special. I stared at the programmes that were not good enough to be put on Christmas day but instead the day afterwards.

I began to contemplate the theory of Christmas but eventually got bored and thought about what the people I knew were doing at this very minute. Eating leftovers, drinking sherry and laughing. I then began to think of what the people I disliked were doing at this very minute. I began to loathe myself.

The concept of Boxing Day is bizarre. It is supposed to be a day in which the family relaxes after a hectic and stressful Christmas. I cannot remember a single Boxing Day where that has happened. Every Boxing Day with my parents ended with a fight. Not a fistfight, instead verbal, but still as vicious. To be lonely is unfortunate but to be lonely on Boxing Day is simply lucky.

I convinced myself that my own profound thoughts were correct in my mind and therefore decided to eat. I cannot cook. There are two types of people; 'cookers', who like to cook and 'orderers', who like to eat pizza. Pizza is my world and I am king of the 'orderers'. I do not know whether it was the knowledge of knowing that someone is giving up their Boxing Day to deliver pizza to me or the fact that I have just lit a cigarette but my hunger had subsided.

This was the first time I had smoked in the house. Claire used to smoke before Emily was born and she just stopped. She also concluded that because she had stopped, I had done as well. I had absolutely no say in the matter. The only problem was that I am not as strong willed as she is. I am not good at anything compared to her. I began to hide. I smoked at work, when I was in the pub and late at night, I would stand outside the house while Claire and Emily were in bed. It was like being fifteen again.

I sat patiently for my dinner. A few minutes later, I stood to get myself a drink. There were four cans of beer in the fridge. I had also hidden a bottle of brandy in my closet for a rainy day. Today it was pouring. I had everything a growing boy needs, alcohol, cigarettes, pizza (arriving soon), and television. For the first time in my five years of marriage, I had become myself again. It is depressing being me.

It was then that I realised that I needed her. I am a woman dependant male. A friend once told me that a break up is like mourning a death. Not the death of your partner, but the death of your relationship with your partner. You go through three stages.

Stage One: Denial. This is the initial reaction. You are in shock and you cannot and will not concede to the truth. Stage Two: Depression. You get to the stage where you lose control and eventually, it can lead to despair. Stage Three: Acceptance. And then you move on.

I convinced myself that I was in stage three. Who am I trying to fool? I am the king of stage one. I am beginning to like stage one because I know eventually, I am going to have to venture into stage three. I was concocting plans to skip stage two and suddenly the doorbell rang.

Food. Wonderful food. The king of stage one was to eat his royally prepared banquet of pizza and rule his kingdom of loneliness. I am too engrossed to think. I changed the channel to wrestling. Another no-no on Claire's list of things that I am not allow to do. Three hours of non-stop world wrestling action. I digress.

The fun stops and I had become drunk. I decide to sleep on the sofa. My sofa.

january

The rays of the sun crashed through the cracks of the canopy and onto the forest bed. I wandered through this lonely deep forest in search of raw preservation but found genuine passion. For the first time in my life, I had felt one with the organic trance of the forest.

The immersed brown of the forest bed merged with the lush greens of the trees. The scent of flowers surrounded me. The acres of dense woodland made me feel peaceful rather than alone. I sat quietly under an immense tree.

I was in absolute bliss. This rapture had become my seventh heaven. I rested until the sky grew dark. I began to appreciate every minute of life. This was beyond any Shangri-la. The trees towered over me like walls. Stop. Stop reading this. If you are expecting a deep analogy of elevated diction or complex syntax, then I suggest you put this book down. Read a best seller. Read the Guardian. Enjoy the multifaceted lexis of Hemmingway.

This stream of consciousness looks at the idea of the broadening of one's mind and achieving ambition. I am, as she put it, 'full of crap'. I have spent the last week sleeping on the sofa. The idea of waking up and not having Claire beside me was much to bear. I had decided to take some time off work to recover. I do not think they have actually noticed yet.

My name is Vincent Thomas. I am twenty-six and I am a financial advisor. I am separated from my wife and I have a five-year-old daughter called Emily. I live in Dublin, Ireland. I am not actually Irish, I moved to this wonderfully wet island six years ago when I got married. Claire wanted to be close to her mother. Her father passed away a year before she met me. She never talked about it.

Emily on the other hand loves to talk. She could talk for England. At five she is already more intelligent than I am. We like the same cartoons and we occasionally team our efforts to anger my esteemed ex-partner. Emily is great. I never thought I would ever be a father. It is amazing that someone so small could change your life forever. The thought of losing Emily was driving me crazy. I had problems with it at first. It is something you never really get used to.

The prospect of work today was inconceivable. I did not want to sit behind a computer for ten hours. I wanted to lie down. Stay in bed all day. Not move. I did not want to be a financial advisor. I have spent a lot of time pondering this, if they started showing ER when I was a teenager, I probably would have become a doctor. But instead they showed Cheers and I became a drinker.

One ambition I had was to write. When I was twenty, I began to write a novel about this guy in a forest. It started really well but I got bored and concluded that I wanted to spend my university years drinking.

While reminiscing, I decided that I wanted to spend the day in bed. I had not really slept properly on the sofa and the bed seemed to appeal to me. Our, sorry, my bedroom was very simple. Claire wanted to have a trendy house. She used to give me the 'less is more' speech that always seemed to confuse me. The walls were white and we had wooden flooring. The bed was made of chrome and had white sheets. There was a colossal bay window, which had white curtains drawn across. It looked like something out of an Argos catalogue.

I lay silently. I was waiting for something to happen. But nothing happened. No-one shouting at me and telling me to get out of bed. No hyperactive five-year-old trying to describe me a toy they have seen on television. It was perfect.

I lied. I hate this. The silence becomes unbearable. I scream. The good city of Dublin heard nothing. I began to feel tearful. I was thinking of my wedding day. Not the actual wedding day but the video of the wedding day. It was like people being nostalgic in films. I did not bother calling in sick. It would have made no difference. I think you get to a certain point and things that would usually concern you become obliterated into the bigger picture.

I work for a major accounting firm in the centre of Dublin. There is a Starbucks on our ground floor and a McDonalds less than five minutes away. I am the envy of all my middle class friends. I live in a luxury, executive flat that has a great view of a construction site. My job is simple. I tell grown up rich kids how to make more money. I have my own office, which has a sofa, my own computer that I will eventually learn how to use. I also have an assistant who cannot stand me.

Kevin, my assistant is waiting for me to die so he can have my job and more importantly, my sofa. Kevin began working there when he was sixteen. It was a work experience fiasco and he just stayed. For the last three years, he has been my assistant. He knows how I drink my tea and knows when to leave me alone. We have a good relationship.

My manager or 'team leader' as William likes to be known is 'married to his job', as he eloquently put it at the last staff party. He works from seven in the morning until ten at night. According to some of the cleaners, he has been known to spend the night at work to do some number crunching. He invited me to play golf with him once but I do not think he actually plays. He just wanted to make conversation.

The building stands at the corner of Fitzroy Street, which is about five minutes away from where I live. I have to wake up at around half past eight to get to work for nine. The stench of Christmas is still in the flat. The tree I created is still standing strong. I open a window and bury myself back into the white duvet.

The feeling of waking up after midday makes me a little disorientated. The wind grew colder so I arose to close the window. I made myself some tea and ran a bath. I had enough sleep to be scientifically described as a coma. It was time I ventured to the outside world. I had also run out of liquor. Before you get the wrong idea about me, I am not an alcoholic. Alcoholics go to meetings; I am merely in stage two. Good old depression.

Claire leaving has left a hole. If you rub your stomach, there is an area, which feels, either content or unbelievably empty. I assume this is what it is like to be my supervisor, William. I think I will take him up on his golf offer. The bath is full of hot soapy water. I do not usually have baths. I prefer showers. I decide to use some of Claire's bath oil. My judgement was poor because now all I can smell is lavender, which reminds me of Claire.

The bathroom, again in Ikea white, was Claire's sanctuary. It had many girly things in it. Bath oils, Body Shop shampoos, and lotions with extremely peculiar names. I sat content in the aroma of Claire and decided to play with Emily's rubber duckie. I think I played with it more than she did. With the rubber duck in my hand, I did not know whether to giggle or cry. I sat patiently in the bath. After a couple of hours, I decided that it was time to stop bathing and get dressed.

I never have problems deciding on what to wear. Today however was different. My blue jeans and brown suede boots are rudimentary. But do I wear the black sweatshirt or the grey University of Reading tee shirt? It was a tough decision. I decided not to be pretentious and just wear black. The colour of mourning.

I grabbed my keys from the kitchen table and grabbed my coat. It was actually my suit jacket because my coat was at the dry cleaners. Emily decided she was going to be sick on me for no reason. Claire did not tell me what dry cleaners she went to. Maybe she met somebody there? She met a guy who was taking his Armani suit to the cleaners and they got talking. One thing led to another… I need to get out of the house.

I got into the lift and pushed the bottom button. There was nobody in the lift because they were all at work, where I should be. I had a little flashback of my mother making me feel bad for missing school. My mother was a travel agent for guilt trips. I was interrupted by the sound of the bell in the lift. I had arrived into the outside world. I walked casually through the lobby. I could feel the neighbours' eyes on me, looking at my unshaven skin and my mourning black attire.

The light of the outside world hit my face like a firework. It was never sunny in Ireland. The second of January is always regarded as the most depressing day in the year. I felt the full brunt of it. The air was thick with dread. People wanted more time off. It became unbearable. I walked the five minutes to get to the supermarket.

This was the first time in a while I went shopping without Emily. It was unnerving not hearing the 'I want' chant while shopping. I headed straight for the alcohol section. I bought some cheap wine and a bottle of Jack. Satisfied with my choice I stormed to the checkout. While waiting in the queue, I realised how many couples were around me. I tried giving myself the 'I earn more money than these people' speech in my head but it just made me feel even worse.

The woman looked at me when I got to the till. A large old lady, she did not want to talk and neither did I so we just did the purchase ritual and I left. I thought about spending the day walking around and do a little window-shopping. I thought again. Instead, I decided to go home. To my home. It still feels strange saying that.

I opened the front door and the sofa screamed at me. I did not want to upset anybody today so I decided to sit. There was a message on the answering machine. It was my assistant Kevin. He wanted to know where I was. I decided to ring back later when I could explain it to them. I hoped that by then I would be able to explain it to myself. Kevin must be in his element. I will execute him if I know he has been sitting on my sofa.

I tried to remember the events of last night or even the last week. I had entered the New Year with absolutely no recollection. How depressing. Still, I have my sofa. I decided that more television, alcohol and delivered pizza are the answers to my problems.

The phone rang. I decided not to get up because I presumed it was work. I heard the 'leave a message' voice that was pre-programmed and then the beep.

'Hello? Vinny? It's Sean. What happened to you last night? Give me a call.' Sean is not Irish. He has an Irish name but he is not from Ireland. In fact, he can be considered anti-Irish. He is the same age as me and he is a chef. His father was a chef, his grandfather was a chef and his brother owns a restaurant. He has a family history of food. He is also my best friend, that is, if you do not include the rubber duckie.

A few days later, Sean appeared at my door with a bottle of Jack. Sean is a big man. He looks a bit like a wrestler but he still has all his teeth. I am sure he still wears spandex when he is alone at home. He looked through the doorway.

'Where are Claire and Emily? Mate, are you okay?' He seemed concerned.

'Come in. I'll tell you all about it.' I mumbled. He came in and opened the curtains. We sat we drank.

It was as if we had not seen each other for years. We talked about what had happened. It felt good to tell somebody.

'Have you been to work?' he still seemed concerned and a little worried.

'No. Not yet. I'm not ready for all that yet.' I was mumbling rather than talking but he was used to it, he was brought up in London.

'Sean, I'm stuck. I really don't know what to do.' I took a deep breath, 'It hurts, it hurts like you wouldn't believe.' He thought about this while finishing his beer.

'Have you left the house?'

'No, well I've been to Sainsburys to get alcohol and cigarettes.'

'Have you spoken to anybody else?'

'Except the duck, no.'

'We're going,' he announced,

'Where?'

'I don't know yet but you're starting to smell like my foot. Go and have a shower and put some clothes on.' He ordered me. I got up and followed procedure. I decided to stay with the mourning attire and put on my black jeans that my mother bought me and the black jumper that Claire brought me. I am a role model for all woman dependant males out there.

I left the flat in a sense of disarray. The taxi Sean ordered while I was mincing around finally arrived. I felt truly cold. We got into the taxi and Sean instructed the driver to go to Temple Bar.

For those that have never been to Temple Bar, it is a small commercial province in the centre of Dublin. This place is like heaven. It is filled with bars, restaurants, hotels and women. Sean paid the driver and we argued over where we were going to eat. I was in the mood for Italian and he wanted Chinese. So we compromised and found a Mexican restaurant. We like Mexican food and tequila seemed like a good idea.

The Mexican restaurant we went into looked as if it was plucked from a small village in Mexico and place into a side street in the centre of Dublin. It was dark, illuminated with only shades of red and green light. The bar appeared frozen in time. We sat and waited for the waitress to serve us.

'So what are you going to do?' Sean asked.

‘Y’know, I have no idea.’

‘Still, it could just be a fight, Michelle and I fight regularly. After an hour or so I just let her win.’

‘I don’t think she’s coming back.’

‘What makes you say that?’

‘I can just tell.’

‘You think there’s someone else?’

‘I do now! Sean! Give me a break.’

‘Look, things like this happen. It’s how long it takes you to get back into the game that determines if you are a man or not.’

‘It just really hurts.’ I tried looking for sympathy but Sean saw through all my self-pity.

‘Pull yourself together Vinny. Be a man and shake it off.’

‘That’s just it, I can’t… I don’t want to.’

‘Then you’re stuck in stage two for a long time.’

‘Just leave it.’

‘No Vinny, you are my friend and after the amount of big brotherly advice you have given me, it seems stupid that I can’t tell you how much of an arsehole you’re being.’

‘Sean, I can’t handle all this now.’

‘Don’t be a loser and move on.’

'Fuck off, Sean.' I got up and left. I could not handle this any more. I was not in the mood for a grilling today. I left the dim restaurant and walked into the street. The rain had stopped. I decided to walk. I heard Sean shout after me but I just kept on going. He did not follow me because we both knew I needed to be alone. Hands in my pockets and head facing the ground I kept walking. The rain began again.

I got home to what seemed like a few days later. I looked at the clock as it hit one o'clock exactly. I decided to sleep and had no problems locating the bed. I had left around fifteen messages on Claire's phone of which about six were audible. I wanted Claire back, I wanted Emily back and I wanted me back. The first couple of weeks of January were the longest I had ever known. Time stood still. I looked out the window and people were walking and communicating. I was neither walking nor communicating. I was sleeping. I was drinking. I was stationary.

The sound of the outside world awakened me and I decided to venture again into the big wide world. I found my work suit and decided that it would be a good idea for me to see if the good people in the accounting department actually missed me.

I arrived at work and was not greeted by anybody. I took the lift to the fourth floor, scurried into my office and sat at my desk. My desk was actually clean. I saw a memo on the table. It was dated about a week ago. 'Vinny, if you decide to come into work at all this year, come up and see me. William.' I closed the door and collapsed on my sofa. I had enough. I wanted to sleep. There was a knock at the door.

'What?!' I shouted.

'It's me, Kevin. Can I come in?' He did not wait for a response and just let himself in.

'What can I do for you, Slick?' I gave him a little nickname every day. He stood there in his matching two-tone shirt and tie. His black trousers that flared at the end and what looked like DKNY shoes. He waved his flop hair away from his eyes. I swear there is an Irish boy band missing a member out there.

'It's William. He wants to see you. I'm going downstairs to get coffee, do you want some?' Do not be fooled by this nice guy approach. He always offers coffee and then simply forgets.

'Yeah, coffee would be good. Is Willy in his office?'

'Yeah.' He replied,

'Okay then sport, go and get coffee and I'll see what William wants.' After my instruction, he left. I collapsed back onto the sofa. After a few minutes pondering on what William wanted, I decided to go and see him.

As I walked through the office, I could see them staring at me, like a pod-person. I knocked on William's door and let myself in. His office was slightly bigger than mine was but he did not have a sofa. It was filled with paperwork and filing cupboards. He was on the phone. It seemed he was trying to get a word into the conversation but every time he started a sentence, it ended up being cut off by the person on the other end.

He eventually stopped talking when he realised that the other person had given up on conversation and put the phone down. He finally got the hint and put down the receiver.

'Vincent, good to see you. Did you have a good Christmas?' He said cheerfully.

'No. Claire left me,' he gave me no reaction but instead, sifted through his paperwork.

'I'm so sorry to her that. Look Vincent, your absence has left me with a problem.'

He cannot sack me. He does not have the balls. 'I'm going to have to let you go.' Suddenly, I was wrong. Maybe he found testicles in his Christmas stocking this year. 'I've argued with the partners but there is nothing I can do. Your notice has already been posted. You can take the rest of the week off.'

I left his office is complete disarray. I had a headache coming on. I saw Kevin in the corner of my eye. Sitting there sucking on his iced coffee. I walked blindly into my office. I gathered a few things, kissed the sofa goodbye and left. I went home and ran myself a bath. It was such a shock that it did not really register until I got home. I realised that I had no case and what they did was actually fair and legally just. I just did not want to accept it. I missed my office already. All I could think about was that little shit, Kevin, getting my job. I began to get angry. There was no way I was going to play golf with him now.

The Christmas tree was beginning to wither. My tree that I created was shrivelling. The house was filled with pizza boxes and the stench of alcohol made it smell like a small brewery. I slept on the sofa at nights and moved to the bed in the mornings. There was no other food in the house. Shaving became a chore and I decided I wanted a beard. I had been wearing the same clothes for a week. I was in shock. And in this chaos, I had found a routine.

I ran the last few weeks over in my head but none of it seemed to make sense. I began to think about religion. Maybe it was because I was not a Catholic and all that crap Claire prescribed to me was actually true. For the first time since I was a child, I prayed. I felt stupid at first but eventually it became part of my routine.

A few days later, I found myself drinking cider because money was tight. There was a knock at the door. I assumed it was the pizza so I grabbed a tenner from the top of the coffee table and walked to the door. It was Sean.

'I'm sorry,' he said.

'Yeah, me too,' I responded. I was glad to see him.

'Look, I should have pushed. I should have...'

'Don't worry about it. You hungry? I've got a pizza coming over.'

'Yeah,' he came in and saw the mess.

'I thought you were supposed to be the clean one. This place is starting to look like my place.'

'I know. I haven't really had time to sort the place out yet.'

'Ah, yes, with your busy schedule and all. How was work?'

'I don't know. I got fired.'

'Seriously? I'm sorry mate. If there is anything I can do.'

'I'm okay.'

'Michelle and I are going on holiday. I just wanted to tell you I'm going to be away for a couple of weeks. Are you going to be okay?'

'Yeah. I'll be fine. Where are you going?'

'Rome.'

'Nice.'

'I'm going to propose to her.' He smiled at me.

'You're kidding. Holy shit! You? The M word.'

'Yeah, I didn't think it was possible either.'

'Well congratulations.' I was genuinely pleased for him. And then, as abruptly as he announced the termination of his free life, there was a knock at the door.

'Pizza,' he said. I got up and answered the door. I collected my pizza in exchange for the tenner and sat back down. We sat for hours, drinking, eating and talking. He left late that night and it felt good. His happiness had transferred onto me. It was time to make a change. Time to move on and do something different.

february

The light of the Venution moons crashed on my face in this mid summer bliss. The realm I had landed on was seamless and unspoiled. The air was warm. I was comforted in thick green leaves. It was home. It was being a baby in a mother's womb.

When I was younger my parents enforced ideas of honesty and trust to propel our relationship. I was allowed the freedom to drink and smoke as I pleased, as long I was honest. Confused, I went along with this absurd request and began to drink and smoke as I pleased.

My friends were constantly reminded that such commodities were wrong. They were forced to hide such endeavours and therefore it seemed more compelling to disobey those who instructed them. Everybody told them that drinking was wrong, they were constantly reminded that by smoking large quantities of tobacco would eventually damage their lungs.

Still, they proceeded. The Government told them it was wrong, their parents and even those false idols created on television were against the idea. Ironically, many of these people smoke and drink regularly. These constant reminders only made them drink and smoke more. I was no longer exempt. I feel the need to smoke twenty a day. By putting age limits on demerit goods, we can inadvertently make things worse. The biggest widespread example of this is drugs. One of the largest trading commodities is in fact illegal.

With Sean in Rome, I found my solace in alcohol and cigarettes. I had thought about an overdose but I decided that I was not cool enough. If I was a rock star and had thousands of fans then maybe I would consider it. And I hate taking pills. Even as a child, I had problems with it.

The great thing about February is that it marks the end of the misery season (Christmas Day, New Years Eve and Valentines Day). The downside to the frosty month of February is that the grandeur of St. Valentines Day divides people into two groups.

Those who are happy in their relationship with their respected partner and those who hide from the parks and other public places in fear of being notorious for being lonely and desperate. I decided to stay home for the whole month.

In the last few weeks, I had decided I was going to change my life. I figured that by April, I would be able to afford to keep this place. I am going to have to sell a few things or look for another job. I decided that a move might be good for me. I did not want to move back in with my parents, partly because I would eventually have to tell them that Claire and I had split up. I love my parents but I did not want to live with them again.

I have given up on television. I decided that I would go back to my books. In the last month, I found a new respect for books. I missed reading. I missed the concentration of my creative subconscious mind. I read until I slept and then read when I woke. I would go through up to four novels a week. My diction improved. I would read in the bath. I would read classics such as Dickens, Bronte and even Shakespeare. I would study philosophy such as Descartes, Socrates and Niche. I even read a couple of Nick Hornby novels. I liked them. One element of Hornby's work is that he did not write for twenty-six year olds but for people who wanted to be twenty-six. It worked, I forgot about the outside world. I became a scholar in my own right.

It was still very cold outside. Claire said she was going to drop Emily over for the weekend. This was the highlight of this frosty month. I cleaned the place up. I threw away the leaning tower of pizza boxes. I hired out her favourite films, Cinderella, George of the Jungle and The Lion King; I was happy with my work and went back to my reading.

The next morning there was a knock at the door. Emily stood there with a big smile on her face. I ushered her in.

'How did you get here?' I asked.

'Mummy dropped me off.' She replied in a soft Irish accent.

'Where is she now?'

'Downstairs,'

'Who is she with?'

'Granny,' I felt relieved. It had been as if a ton of bricks had been lifted from me. I gave her a big emotional hug. Hugging Emily was like cuddling a miniature version of Claire. I asked her if she was having fun at grandma's house.

'I'm not staying at grandma's house; me and mummy are staying at Rob's house.'

'Who's Rob?' I realised what the first heart attack felt like.

'Mummy's friend,' she replied. She ran over to the sofa and pressed play on the remote. I stood there. I felt numb. I could not feel my body. The ton of bricks came crashing back down.

I sat beside her as she cuddled up to me. It was just like when Claire and I watched a film. I sat stationary while transfixed with this little girl. She had long brown hair like Claire. Her green eyes were exact copies of her mother's. And she had a certain grace. I could not explain it. I do not think I want to. It was a mystery and it should be kept that way. We spent a lot of time together. We played on my Playstation and drank sugary drinks, which were not usually allowed.

It was fun. I could not prevent myself from thinking about who this Rob character was. I did not want to grill Emily for information. It did not seem fair. I want Emily to remember me as her friend. It was good to have her at home.

We watched more Disney films; we laughed at the funny parts and cuddled up together during the sad parts. I taught her how to order pizza. She gave me a make-over and did my hair. We drew pictures of each other and made prank phone calls. We had a good time.

Sunday arrived and Claire came to pick her up. Emily picked up her things that I packed for her and sat on the sofa. We watched one of my wrestling videos. And then Claire let herself in. I did not realise she still had a key. She entered the room as she usually did when she walked through the door.

'Come here honey.' Emily reacted immediately and gave her a hug. 'Was she okay?' She asked me. I paused.

'Who's Rob?' I asked not wanting the answer.

'I…uh… Emily, honey, do you want to go to your room and get some things? I'll be there in a minute.' Emily ran up to me and gave me a hug. I gave her a big cuddle and noticed Claire looking away. Emily then left the room and Claire looked at me. She had a hard look that she gave me every time we had an argument.

'He's a friend.' She said, her accent becoming stronger.

'A friend who you are living with,'

'I'm not having this argument with you now,'

'Then when? The day before you get married to this Rob guy.'

'You're being irrational.'

'I am?!'

'Our relationship is like a shark, when a shark stops swimming…'

'…it dies.' I said this without realising it. I knew I should have said something different. She came up to me and put her hand on my shoulder.

'Vinny, we stopped swimming a long time ago.'

'Just give me a minute with Emily.'

'Okay, I'll wait in the lobby.'

Emily came up to me as I went onto my knees. I put my hands on her shoulders. I could sense she knew what was going on.

'I love you,' I said to her.

'I love you too,' she replied. We both had tears in our eyes.

'Look, I know I'm not always going to be around now that your mother and I are not together but that doesn't mean I don't care about you. I love you and I will always be your father.' She began to cry. 'Hey, don't cry. You know the number. Anytime you want to speak to me just pick up the phone and ring me.' She seemed to perk up at this. 'And every couple of weeks we can spend the weekend together and we'll have fun. Just like today.'

'Just like today.' She repeated. They left again. The only exception is that they said goodbye. That night I slept like a baby.

St. Valentine's Day. The one day in the year, you pray that you are in a relationship. As you may have already deduced by now I am experiencing a form of depression. I knew deep down that if I left the house that I could meet new people and possibly find someone who would not leave me for this Rob guy. But I did not want to move on.

I decided to stay in bed for an extra hour today. I eventually rose to find that my day had beckoned. I sat in the living room and watched television. Why change a routine that works? I realised then the one period of television worse than the daytime schedule of programmes, the mid afternoon selection of viewing. I sat and watched an extremely bad game show followed by an entourage of bad eighties repeats. Eventually I found solace in ER, which was showing on a different channel.

We all know that St. Valentine's Day is a con to sell chocolate hearts and roses but year after year, we divulge those who we love in plastic sentiments without, for a minute, contemplating the commercial aspect of these false sentiments. Bitter? Absolutely.

I decided that I would dress today and retrieve more alcohol and cigarettes from the supermarket. I even had a shave. I felt better about myself and decided I would not let this commercial travesty bother me in any way. The outside world was cold and dark. I realised then that I was not the only single person in the world and perked up a little. I almost managed a smile.

The supermarket was filled with more desperate and lonely people. It was like single's night in Sainsburys. I needed some exercise so I strolled through the aisles. I had a couple of impulse buys but eventually ended up in the alcohol section. The prospect of wine appealed to me so I bought a bottle of red and a bottle of white. I am not a wine connoisseur so I did not bother to look for a certain country nor did I select a vintage. I found cheap wine. Along with yet another bottle of Jack and a few beers, I went home.

As I left the supermarket, I saw someone heading towards me. She looked straight at me. Was it? At first, it looked like Claire, but at that moment all women looked like Claire. She had the same hair but this girl was taller. I slowly began to recognise some features. It was that girl from work.

'Vinny Hi,' she said painfully cheerfully.

'Um… Hi.' I could not remember her name.

'How are you? I haven't seen you in the office recently,'

'Err… I… um… quit,' I lied, 'I wanted to take some time off and try something else.'

'Really, I think that is so great. I'm just getting a few things for dinner tonight. I'm cooking dinner for my fiancée,' as she was saying this, I was almost physically sick.

'That's nice,' I could not think of anything else to say.

'How's Claire and Emily,' She asked in a pleasant voice.

'They're fine.' I did not want to go any further than that. I had enough sympathy from everyone else.

'Anyway, I have to go but it was good seeing you.' She began to walk off.

'Yeah, you too.' I lied again. I crept home feeling worse than I ever thought possible.

I got home and I began drinking again. The television was on but the usual mind numbing ritual did not work. Usually when I drink my mind automatically switches itself off after a while but for some reason I began to think more. I thought about Claire and Emily. I pondered the relevance of my life. I reflected on Freud's theory on religion. His deduction that God did not create man but man created God in his own sub-conscious. I considered my parents and for the first time in my life began to think of them as real people. People with lives and feelings.

I needed to change my life. This routine in which I had found consolation was actually annihilating me from the inside. I had become an alcoholic. I stopped drinking from glasses because I could not find the vigour to clean any. I had become a drunk. I loathed myself. I gazed at the half bottle of white wine and threw it against the wall. I screamed. My head felt heavy in my hands. I was disillusioned. I rolled off the sofa and stretched out on the floor. The ceiling seemed a million miles away. I slept.

'Vinny! Vinny, wake up! Shit, Vinny! Open your eyes!' It was like drilling in my head.

'What? What happened?' I saw light. I felt like I had a sumo wrestler using my head as a cushion.

'Oh, thank God, I was worried about you mate.' Sean said in delight.

'Ah, the jolly tanned giant returns.' I smiled. It was good to have Sean back.

'She said yes,'

'What?'

'She said YES!' he was grinning like a five-year-old.

'Congratulations,' I was ecstatic too.

He gave me his hand and he pulled me up on the sofa. He looked good, like a new man.

'You do know that two in every three marriages ends in divorce,' I joked, 'I mean, look at Claire and me…'

'Nothing you can say is going to piss me off,' he was still grinning at this.

It sounds girly but while he was giving me details, we were actually giggling like schoolchildren.

'We took a walk along the side streets. We found a little garden in the middle of all these old buildings. I got on one knee and asked her.'

'Well Casanova, what happened next?'

'We kissed. I mean, we kiss all the time but it was different, I wasn't snogging my girlfriend anymore, I was kissing my fiancée. It was good.'

'I can't believe I'm hearing this from you. This is coming from the man whose philosophy on life was treat them mean, keep them keen.'

'I know,' he laughed, 'but people change,'

'Yeah,'

'Have you heard from Claire?'

'Yeah, she dropped Emily over a couple of days after you left,' our smiles disappeared. We were going into subdued territory.

'She's found someone else,'

'What?' he actually seemed surprised? We both knew it was logical but it was still a jolt to the system.

'Yeah, I confronted her about it but got nothing.'

'Did you really want details?'

'Not really,'

'Are you okay?' Sean had a big brother character he would assume when things like this happened.

'Not sure. I'm still breathing,'

'Look, I'm here for you amigo.'

'I know,'

'What happened there?' Sean pointed to the smashed bottle of wine against the wall.

'I decided to give up alcohol,'

'Do you see what I mean about change?'

'Yeah,' I smiled. 'Sean, I'm in a mess. What do I do?'

'Well, you're starting to smell like my foot again so I think you should go and sort yourself out.' His affirmation inspired me to break my routine.

'C'mon, I'll buy you dinner.'

As we left the taxi, we headed for the main square in Temple Bar. We had our ritual argument about where we were going to eat. I was in the mood for Indian and he fancied Thai. On our way to the Mexican restaurant, we passed many couples.

'Even the day after Valentine's Day, this place is full of couples.' I announced.

'Mate, Valentine's Day was two days ago,' Sean looked at me slightly startled.

'You're kidding, please tell me your messing around with me,' I looked at my watch and found to my dismay that it was the sixteenth.

'Have you thought about seeing a doctor?' He smiled. I laughed. I knew that was my last binge and the idea of alcohol now repulsed me. We ate enchiladas and I had a coke. The idea of going to a restaurant and not drinking did not feel as peculiar as I initially thought it would.

'So, have you thought about what you're going to do?' Sean asked.

'Not yet. I've been considering a move.'

‘Where?’

‘I haven’t figured that bit out yet.’

‘Good plan,’

‘Don’t start,’ he became sarcastic when he was happy, ‘I was thinking the homeland,’

‘England? Move back in with your parents?’

‘God no, I was thinking London,’

‘That dump? Why?’

‘I don’t know, I’ve always wanted to live in a big city but I don’t want to be too far away from Emily. I’m bored with Ireland, I don’t fit in here. London seems like a good change of scenery.’

‘Have you actually been to London?’

‘Once, when I was younger, my parents took me to see the sights. It seemed like a nice place,’

‘Being a tourist in London is different,’

‘I know, but the idea of it seems really…

‘…Stupid?’

‘No, cool.’

‘Let me get this correct, you want to move to a different city because it seems cool?’

‘I can’t stay here anymore. Being in Dublin is killing me. Everything here reminds me of her.’

'Look, you're my best friend so I'm going to help you,' It was bizarre seeing Sean being so serious. 'My brother, James, owns a restaurant in Earls Court. He lives above it and he has a spare room. I'll talk to him.'

'Sean, I appreciate it but don't put yourself out, plus, I haven't really decided on anything yet.'

'What are you going to do when you get there?' It was as if he chose to ignore what I just said and launched into an odd excitement.

'I don't know. Find a job?'

'What, doing what you did here?'

'No. Something different,' I looked around the restaurant as I said this. Surprisingly the bottle of Jack Daniels behind the bar did not call out at me.

'Like…'

'I don't know. Something,'

'Do me a favour, sleep on it.' I smiled as he said this. We left the restaurant. I felt better. I felt sober. We walked back to my flat because we both ate a little too much. On the way, we talked about the wedding. We passed an abundance of closed shops on our return. The streets were actually quite empty for Temple Bar. As we walked past Waterstones, I stopped.

'What is it?' Sean asked.

'Look,' I pointed inside the window. Sean pushed his nose against the window.

'What am I looking at?' He quizzed.

'That,'

'What?'

'Books,' as I said this he looked at me.

'Are you still drunk from two days ago?' he smiled.

'No, I want to be a writer,'

'You're kidding?'

'No. I'm serious. I don't think I've ever been this serious about anything. I'm going to be a novelist.'

'C'mon, it's late. We better get back.' He kept his smile. We did not discuss it on the way back but it was all I could think about. Sean decided he was going to stay the night. He rang Michelle and we sat up late watching the music channels on cable.

The whole time I kept reviewing the idea of being a novelist. The idea remained in the back of my mind.

'I want to get married in Vegas,' Sean declared with a juvenile grin. I laughed. 'I want Elvis as my priest!' We both laughed uncontrollably. We were both on a high from the evening.

'And you can have Love Me Tender playing while Michelle walks down the aisle,' I added, we laughed harder. He drank beer and I smoked cigarettes. I decided that I would continue to smoke as a sign of rebellion.

Sean woke me before he left. I decided to do a little retail therapy. I went and bought clothes, books and CDs. I specifically bought items that I knew I usually would not be allowed. It was the first time this year I walked through Dublin with my eyes open. My despair had been turned to hope. I had let my hair grow, put on a little weight and grown a slight beard.

I walked into HMV and bought heavy metal albums and Fight Club on DVD. I had breakfast in McDonalds and did not feel guilty about it. I was pampering myself. For the first time in a while I was being myself. I bought more books from Waterstones and sat in the park. I spent an hour in Next buying a new wardrobe, buying clothes that I usually would not wear. On my return, I stopped by a jeweller and looked through the window. I decided to get my left ear pierced. The twelve-year-old girl that was performing my earlobe surgery appeared nervous; hence, it scared the living daylight out of me. Eventually I calmed down and she put the piercing gun next to my ear. It was over in moments and all that remained was a sense of revolution.

I got home and cleaned my house. I put tasteful posters in the frames of paintings that Claire put up. I played with my hair and had a shave. I located my purchases and put them in action. I was a new man; smart, powerful and sexy. Finally, I opened the curtains. The time for change was afoot.

march

My insatiable need for thirst prevailed. I decided to wander the forest in exploration of water. I drifted through the immense plantation observing the peculiar creatures that inhabited this breathtaking planet. Creatures I could never have fathomed. These gracious and forthcoming creatures did not appear ferocious but continued to subsist in the rapture of their planet.

I was woken by a thunderous knock at the door. I lay in bed hoping that the hellacious noise would disappear. It did not. In silent rage, I threw off the bed covers and proceeded towards the door. The incessant thumping continued.

'WHAT!' I bellowed with my eyes barely open. I saw Sean looking at me with a look of confusion.

'Michelle's pregnant,' Sean looked intently at me as he said this.

‘Come in,’ I said in a calm manner. He entered the room like a giant and collapsed on the sofa. I put a music channel on and I looked at him. He gave the impression that he was worried. I have never seen Sean worried.

‘I’m going to be a dad,’ he uttered. ‘I don’t know the first thing about being a father.’

‘It’s not that bad,’ I tried to reassure him.

‘It’s different. You’re good at being a dad. You’re the dad type, what am I going to do with my child? Take it drinking?’ I laughed as he said this.

‘Sorry,’ I paused, ‘I think you’d be a good father,’

‘Really?’

‘Yeah, you’ll pick it up. I was twenty-one when Claire and I had Emily. I was still paying off my student loan when she was born and we’re okay. The first few months are tough but you’ll get through it. Everyone does.’

‘Michelle told me I have to marry her soon. I don’t think her Catholic parents are too keen on the idea of pre marital sex,’

‘When?’

‘I don’t know, I was thinking of the summer,’ and then looked at me, ‘Will you be my best man?’

'Of course, of course I will,' I hugged him. Sean and I rarely hug but this was a hugging moment.

'There's a problem, Claire's going to be there,'

'I guessed, she being Michelle's best friend,' I said in a sarcastic tone.

'That won't bother you?'

'Nah, I'll be okay,' I felt confident, I was a new person.

'Okay, now we've got that out the way, I'm going to have to take the piss out of your ear ring.'

'Leave me alone,' I smiled.

'Okay Captain Pugwash, you can come to the wedding but the ear ring has to stay at home.'

'Deal, now will you leave me alone?'

'Yeah, I've got to go anyway, I'll give you a ring,' and then he left. I was going to be a best man. I was getting over Claire. I had reached stage three, acceptance.

With my new-found acceptance, I remained awake. I made myself a hearty breakfast and watched the news. After a quick shower, I dressed in my new clothes and looked in the mirror. I felt good. I decided to take a walk.

I left the lobby in an excellent frame of mind and advanced to the art gallery. I recollect driving past the art gallery on a daily basis each time pledging that I would one day make a visit. Today was that day. I spent an hour looking at post modernistic styles, assessing them with the contemporaries. I had no idea what I was doing but it felt good nonetheless.

I had lunch in a trendy bistro and read a Dick Francis novel. For the first time in my life I felt cultured. I experienced an urge to listen to classical music and drink fine wine. I spent the week redecorating the apartment. I put candles ubiquitously around the apartment. I put my posters in frames and put up a wine rack.

On Sunday, I rang Claire's mother asked to speak to Claire. I knew she would be there because she always goes to her mothers after mass.

'Vinny, I don't want you ringing me here,' she said firmly down the phone.

'I just wanted to know if I could have Emily this weekend.'

'Um... yeah... you'll have to pick her up though.'

'No problem, where do you live now?'

'From my mother's house, Vinny,'

'Oh, okay, so be it.' I felt like a five-year-old. 'When? What time?'

'Friday, around six.'

'Okay, no problem. Listen, I think it's great…' Then she hung up. She cut me off while I was trying to be mature and civil. This means war. I wanted to find out why she really left me. I wanted to know who Rob is. I needed answers.

As Sean's best man, I had to attend the engagement party. I knew Claire would be there so it had become my mission to look my best. I wanted her to feel bad. I then realised I had gone back to my denial phase. Back to stage one. I stared up at the ceiling trying to decide which tie would make my wife return to me. I resolved with the blue. After spending an hour in bath and soaping myself with an entire bottle of hand wash, it became apparent that I was not as good looking as I used to be.

I looked in the mirror and saw an old man. Withered with age desperately trying to get his life back; I looked at my new beer belly that I had acquired and felt the presence of more hair than I thought I'd ever have. I brushed my teeth, shaved and coated my skin in the aftershave that Claire bought me for my birthday. After spending a few minutes playing with my hair, I put on my black suit and black shirt and looked again in the mirror. I could still see the frail old man underneath.

I arranged for a taxi to collect me and lingered in the hallway for the lift to take me to the lobby. As I entered the lift, I noticed an attractive young lady. She had lengthy brown hair and green eyes, which were apparent in most Irish women, and she smiled at me. I had not been smiled at in four years. I may have done but never really noticed it because I was besotted with Claire. Eventually I smiled back. The attractive girl gave me a seductive look.

The lift stopped moving, the doors exposed the lobby, and the girl walked off. I decided to follow her. A bulky man wearing a tight white tee shirt came to greet her. I decided I would let this one go and headed to the outside world. I lit a cigarette while waiting for my taxi.

Eventually, the taxi halted outside of Sean's house. I gave my fare to the disgruntled driver and marvelled at my friend's home. I knocked on the door and Michelle answered. She screeched my name and gave me a big hug. It became obvious that I was the only sober person in the house. I performed the duty of reacquainting myself with everybody and introduced myself to some new individuals that may have stumbled to the wrong party.

'Vinny!' I heard a very excited voice shout.

'Sean!' I repeated in the same tone.

'Congratulations!'

'Thanks mate, can I get you a drink?'

'Yeah, orange juice if you've got any,'

'No problem, comrade,' He smiled as he walked off. I spent an hour talking to people I have been avoiding since Claire left me. We discussed everything from the weather to the Rolling Stones. We did not however discuss the last three or so months. Everyone acted as if nothing had happened. I found this quite comforting; I did not want sympathy, especially from these people. The doorbell rang and I faced my inevitability, I had to encounter them together. I had to watch them hold hands and kiss. I had to listen to their stories and their plans for the future. I did not want to congregate any more. I decided to leave, go home and hide under my bed covers.

'Claire! Hi!' Michelle got over excited again, 'Rob, good to see you again,' I was dreading this moment, the moment he walks through that door. The theory behind this was insane; I had arrived to a party with my wife and her new boyfriend. I belonged on Jerry Springer. I took a deep breath. My mind blanked out all sounds. It was silent.

Then it happened. A blond, scarf wearing Brad Pitt wannabe entered the room, his hand holding Claire's hand. I felt sick. I wanted the ground to swallow me up. I held back the tears and began to plan my escape. I could see her looking at me. I walked into the kitchen and opened the back door. As I left, I could hear some commotion.

I walked down the road like a little boy who left home for the first time. I could hear someone running after me. I closed my eyes hoping it was Claire. I wanted this bad dream to be over. I looked around. It was Sean, he had realised that I had gone.

'Hey, Vin, you okay?'

'Yeah, I… uh… realised I had left the oven on and…'

'C'mon man, you knew she was gonna be here,'

'Yeah, I thought I was ready,' I was still holding back the tears, 'Look, you better go back, you're going to miss your engagement party.'

'This is more important,'

'No really, I just need to be alone,'

'You sure?' He smiled.

'Yeah, I've got to go and switch my oven off anyway,'

'Okay, I'll ring you tomorrow,'

'Yeah, have fun,' I said this without any resentment. I knew he did not want Claire and her new puppy at his party but he had no choice. I walked home to get some perspective and get some air.

I got home in the early hours of the morning. I went to my room and collapsed on the bed. I reached for the remote and put on some heavy metal music. I looked at the ceiling and put every effort into closing my eyes. After a few minutes, I let it out. I screamed. I made as much noise as my lungs would let me. Anger management was not my strong point. I looked at a picture of us on the dressing table. I stood near it and with one sudden blow it exploded onto the floor. I was now in a destructive mood. I gathered all the things we bought together and hurtled them against the wall. The CDs we bought together, souvenirs from holidays we had been on and finally my wedding ring. I rummaged around the apartment like a thief.

My rage eventually led me to a bottle of Jack that I hid behind the cereals in one of the kitchen cupboards. I cried and I drank. I became docile and accepted my fate. The prodigal son had returned to stage two; depression.

The following day I awoke at what seemed to be mid afternoon. I tried to look at the clock Claire and I bought from Ikea but it was now a shattered mess on the floor. Time had now stood still. The phone rang and I eventually answered it.

'Hey buddy, are you okay?' Asked Sean's familiar voice,

'Um… yeah… I think so.'

'Okay, I was thinking I'd drop by and spend some time with you.'

'Yeah, yeah, great,' I mumbled

'I'll be round in about half an hour.'
I looked around the apartment. It looked like Ozzy Osbourne's hotel room after a sold out concert. I tried to summon the energy to clean but instead returned to bed. I could not move. The world was spinning around me. I felt unwell mentally and physically. The image of them holding hands killed me.

Eventually I heard a knock at the door.
'It's open,' I tried to scream but for some reason my voice had gone. Sean entered.
'Hello, how are… what happened?' The shock set in and he froze. 'Vinny, what the…?
'Close the door,' I mumbled; the enormity of the situation finally hit me,
'Are you okay?'
'Yeah, bit of a mess, huh?' I joked.
'No shit, what happened?'
'I think I got drunk,'
'I thought you gave up?'
'Yeah, it wasn't a conscious decision.'
'C'mon, let's clear up,'

'Yeah,' I was glad I had Sean as a friend. We did not talk much while cleaning up but I could sense he felt for me. We began with the kitchen and then the living room. I had managed to break everything of some value in the flat. We discarded broken plates, a mirror and some household ornaments. I was cleansing myself from things I had depended on for a long time.

The only thing that was in tact was my beloved sofa and my television. These things belonged to me. Claire had no claim to them because I had them before I met her. I had stripped myself to the essentials. Sean used his mobile phone to order a pizza because I had jumped on my house phone during my fit of rage. After frantically cleaning the place, we eventually sat down and relaxed.

'Not much left,' Sean vocalised his observations.

'It was all crap I didn't need.' I felt like the Zen master when I said this.

'Suit yourself but promise me this, next time you do this, wait 'til I leave the country,' He smiled. I lit a cigarette.

'What's Rob like?'

'Pretentious arsehole,'

'Really?' I felt better.

'Pretty much, he's an utter wanker,' Sean put on his cockney accent as he said this.

'So what you're saying is that my wife left me for a wanker?' I tried saying this with a straight face. We laughed. It is funny how we joke about things that have hurt us emotionally. The pizza arrived and Sean paid for it.

'Sean, I've been thinking, I'm finding it really hard living here and soon my lease is going to expire,'

'Yeah,' Sean uttered with his mouthful of pizza.

'I'm moving,' I paused. Silent. 'Sean, I'm leaving Dublin,'

'Where are you going to go?'

'London,'

'I thought you were joking,'

'No, I've had some time to think about it and it seems like a good idea.'

'Listen, if you feel you have to do this then I'm completely behind you.'

'Thanks,' we watched some television. It only occurred to me then that I was going to miss this.

The idea of moving still appeared positive but I would be leaving a good friend behind.

'Do you want me to ring my brother?' Sean asked.

'About?' I thought I missed a conversation.

'About the flat in Earls Court. I can ask him to put you up until you get yourself sorted.'

'Nah, don't worry about it,'

'London is a lonely place. When I lived there I didn't even meet my neighbours and I lived there for ten years.'

'Okay, but if he cannot then don't worry about it,' after I said this we became engrossed with the pizza. Sean then turned to me and asked,

'Have you thought about what you're going to do when you get there?'

'Um… I was thinking about writing,'

'Are you joking?'

'No. what's wrong with that?'

'London's also expensive; you're going to need a job,'

'I'll worry about that when I get there,' I tried to appear confident but the truth was I was scared. After Sean left, I thought about what he said. I got dressed and took a trip to my local Internet café. I attempted a little research and booked my plane ticket with British Airways. I found a company that would collect what remained of my possessions and keep them in storage. I wrote down numbers that I may need and enjoyed a large mocha.

I spent the rest of the week arranging my belongings in cardboard boxes and organising storage of items I did not need. It felt strange. I moved into this flat while in love with my wife. We had a beautiful daughter and I made lots of money. In a few days, I will be on my own, living in a city I have only been to once and I will probably be working in a restaurant.

I think it is humorous the way we are dealt cards and the possibility of our worlds changing around us. The interesting thing in this is that we have no control over what happens. I believe in fate, I believe things happen for a reason. It is only when we are exposed to that reason that we truly comprehend the beauty of our own existence.

I am not afraid to illustrate my fear of change but I will however embrace it and follow my calling regardless how turgid and difficult the journey may be. It is time to accept that my fate has changed.

What I assumed would last forever, will only be a nostalgic reflection on what could have been.

That evening I shed a tear for this old apartment. Our home, our sanctuary had fallen into the demise of transformation. I reflected on the memories we shared and found comfort in the simple truth that I had been fortunate to experience such wonder. The reality is that you honestly do not know what you have until it has gone. This lyric actually made sense now. I was now to face new challenges and discover a new familiarity from my life.

april

I stumbled upon a great waterfall; the forest succumbed to an oasis of tremendous beauty. This splendour eclipsed the rays of the various suns. I was blinded by the magnificence of this streaming cascade. I was lured by a thirst. I cupped my hand and drank the shimmering clear water. My thirst had been quenched.

The first week of April was fraught with tasks and emotional complications. I sat on my sofa marvelling at the emptiness; the empty white walls and the sullen floor, which once held the remains of family life. The thought of this carpet made me ponder the contemplation that I may never walk on it again. In less than a month, it will have new feet to tread on it. New lives with new complications.

I had the help of my friend Sean, while carefully placing extracts of my life in cardboard boxes marked fragile. I sensed he was a little upset when the reality finally caught up with him. My time had come; change was inevitable. I decided to treat myself to breakfast. I walked to a little café I used to go to. It seemed like I had not been there for years.

The chime dangled as I opened the door, it was not full. I sat and observed the menu even though I knew what I wanted. The waitress came over to me to take my order. She must have been sixteen with a look of despair on her face. Her eyes were red and her skin was pale. She could be stunning but there was something stopping her.

I ordered the full Irish breakfast, which was a blatant replica of the full English breakfast. My fresh orange juice arrived early and I sipped slowly and occasionally. I found a paper and began to read the stories I did not find depressing or morbid. Instead of reading about a rapist on the lose or war breaking out in Iraq; I read stories about people who had made a difference, the woman who gave birth to eight children, or the story of the pensioner who sky dived at the tender age of eighty seven.

My mid afternoon breakfast finally arrived. I chewed through the crisp, hot bacon. I sliced the grilled tomato and ate it with my succulent sausage. I punctured the yolk of my egg and watched it trickle down the fried bread. After I ravished my breakfast, I sat and gazed at my surroundings. It was a small place with bright pine furniture and pictures of flowers on the magnolia walls. The counter was positioned near the back of the restaurant and four women were busying themselves with several tasks at once. It was cosy.

I glared through the window into the outside world. I observed people walking past. I watched the cars rush by and felt at ease in the warmth. I paid my bill at the counter and left. It would be the last time that I had a full Irish breakfast. I walked back via Waterstones and bought a Bill Bryson novel. I returned home to my daybed and began to read.

I found myself laughing the entire evening, even though I was in a sober state. The thought of moving to London had not crossed my mind until late at night when I ordered a pizza. I contemplated the theory that with my moving away, I may put the pizza company out of business. I thought about the theorem in which it is hypothesised that if a butterfly flaps its wings in the Atlantic then there would be a tornado in China. What if I was that butterfly? I pondered the repercussions of my actions. I realised then that the person I would most affect was Emily. I knew I could see her when I wanted to and the flight was reasonably cheap but something ate away at me. I needed closure from Claire and needed to say goodbye to Emily.

The day had finally arrived for my voyage to the great city of London. I felt both excited and petrified as I woke that morning. The sun hit through the thin white curtains of my room. I decided today that I would visit Emily. Since Claire and I had separated, we came to the agreement that I could have Emily on alternate weekends. Emily and I ring each other on regular basis. I knew our relationship would never be the same. I remember Claire proclaiming something when Emily said 'Daddy' for the first time. Anybody can be a father; it takes someone special to be a dad. I know I am not a bad father but in truth, I felt like I was abandoning my daughter.

I knew Claire would be staying with her mother. I arrived at her mother's house by taxi and found comfort in the fact that Rob was not there. I confronted Claire immediately. She looked at me as if I was inconsequential to her.

'I'm moving away,' I said bluntly,

'Where?' She seemed a little concerned

'London.'

'London? What are you going to do in London? I thought you hated London?'

'No, you hated London; I need a new environment,'

'Okay, whatever. When are you going?'

'Today, that's why I came over. I wanted to say goodbye to you and Emily,'

'I better go and get her,' she spoke in a cold-hearted manner, 'Emily, come and talk to daddy,'

'Dad?!' I could see her running down the stairs. I realised that this was not going to be easy. My eyes began to fill with tears. I hugged her and asked Claire to give us a few minutes. I knelt on the floor in front of her in the foyer.

'Emily, I want you to know I love you, I have to go away,'

'Where?'

'London,'

‘When are you coming back?’

‘I’m going to be living there, I’ll come back to visit you and you can come and stay with me.’

‘I want you to stay here,’

‘I can’t honey, I love you. Give me a hug,’ and with that tearful speech she held onto me and did not let go. I could see Claire watching us from the corner of my eye. ‘I’ll ring you every other day, I promise.’ I stood weeping. ‘I have to go; I’m going to miss my flight. I’ll ring you from the airport. I love you.’ And with that, I left. I knew I would see my daughter again but never in the same way. I promised myself I would always be her dad and never just her father.

The taxi was still waiting outside with my luggage. I returned to the car and asked the driver to take me to the airport. I looked back and saw Emily waving at me. That image will never leave my mind.

I sat in the back of the taxi wiping my eyes and trying to compose myself. I rested my head against the cold glass.

‘It’s always hard to say goodbye,’ a sudden voice came from the front.

'I'm sorry?'

'Saying goodbye, it's very emotional,'

'Yeah,' I did not know how to reply to this stranger,

'I had to say goodbye to my little girl once,'

'Really?' I thought I would humour his conversation.

'Yeah, it's tough. I haven't seen my daughter for six years now,'

'I'm sorry,'

'Don't be. It's better to have happily separated parents rather than unhappily married parents.'

'You're right, I just wish…'

'…Don't bother wishing what could have been, worry about the future,'

'Yeah, thanks. My names Vinny by the way,'

'Adam, I'd shake your hand but we'd crash,' he laughed as he said this, 'So what do you do Vinny?'

'Um… not sure yet, writer I think,'

'Really, what have you written?'

'Nothing as yet, I'm getting around to it,'

'So where are you going?'

'The airport,'

'I know that, where from the airport?'

'London,' I said affirmatively. Adam's phone rang. It was not a business call. He chirped away happily while I stared out the window. I felt like I was six again. I watched as the trees on the side of the road whisked by. I stared at the other cars trying to determine the type of people that would drive them. The taxi was relatively new and unlike most Dublin cabs, this was white. Adam was a large man wearing driving gloves and an Irish rugby shirt.

'Sorry about that,' He said,

'Don't worry about it,' I smiled as I replied. We talked for the rest of the ride and watched as the sun vanished into the clouds. I felt unusually nervous as we entered one of the Dublin airport terminals. Adam and I exited together. I paid him and he collected my suitcases.

'Thanks for the ride,' I said,

'No problem,' Adam replied, 'look after yourself,'

'I will,' he waved goodbye and I nodded in return. I checked in and found my plane had been delayed for half an hour. I sat in the airport coffee bar and devoured a blueberry muffin with my cappuccino. I began to observe my surroundings; I watched a couple kissing waiting to go on that city break, I noticed a business man in his Armani suit frantically going through paperwork and a family arguing about whose fault the plane was delayed.

I heard the boarding call and grabbed my hand luggage. I watched as everyone scurried to get on the plane as if it would leave them behind. I found my seat and sat patiently in anticipation on who would sit next to me. Then I conjured up the perfect plan and slept. I used to love meeting new people but recently I have become a little reclusive.

I was awakened an hour later by the sound of the air-hostess dragging her trolley down the walkway. I ordered an orange juice and rested my head back into my seat. I found myself sitting next to the happy couple as they held hands. I closed my eyes again and listened to the drivel that was in-flight entertainment. I have never been good on aeroplanes and began to feel a little claustrophobic. I turned on the air conditioning and closed my eyes. After falling back to sleep for what seemed like ten minutes, I was woken again by the smell of aeroplane cuisine. I decided not to eat and tried to nod off.

The two-hour flight lasted for what seemed a day. I alighted from the craft and headed for the terminal to hopefully retrieve my luggage. I lit a cigarette, which felt, like my victory for surviving the plane trip from hell. I looked at the cold darkness outside while in expectancy of my luggage. After smoking my cigarette, I collected my luggage and hailed a taxi to Earls Court. I had written the address of James's restaurant on a piece of paper and I handed it to the driver.

I arrived at the restaurant later that day when most people were at home. I was slightly nervous. I was being accepted into a stranger's home and felt indebted to Sean's brother. During the journey, for no explicable reason, I kept forgetting James' name.

The taxi driver had dropped me off down the road from the restaurant because traffic was heavy. I walked along until I saw the most exquisite little Italian restaurant, the sign above it was a wooden plaque and had 'Little Italy' inscribed in gold. I peered through the window and saw that it went back a long way.

I entered and an attractive tanned woman greeted me. She looked like an extra from the Godfather; she had stunning olive skin and silky hair. I was beginning to adore this place already.

'I'm here to see James,' I said feeling like an immigrant,

'You must be Vinny,' she replied in a heavy cockney accent, the dream was over,

'Yeah, is he here?' I asked,

'No, but he will be soon, are you hungry?'

'Actually, yes,'

'I'll get you a table, relax,'

'Okay, thanks,' She took my luggage and I sat at a table. She wandered off into the kitchen and I lit a cigarette. The walls were a golden brown with large pictures of scenic Italy affixed to them. The restaurant was very authentic and distributed around were plants. It seemed very organic. The charming little bar was located on the right hand side and the tables went back quite far.

'Hey, I'm Kate.' The attractive woman reached over to shake my hand. I immediately stood up,

'I'm Vinny,'

'Was your trip okay?'

'Yeah,'

'I've just rung James and he's running a little late, can I get you a drink?'

'Yeah, can I have an orange juice?'

'No problem, I'll bring one over,' I sat and admired this sanctuary of food until she came back. Kate. She did not look like a Kate. Catherina maybe, Bella would suit her but not Kate. She returned with two glasses of orange juice and came to sit with me.

'Won't you get in trouble for sitting during your shift?' I questioned,

'Why, don't you want me sitting with you?'

'No no, no I don't mind, I just...'

'I'm kidding, the boss is away,' she replied.

'Oh,' there was a slight uncomfortable pause, 'So how long have you worked here?'

'Pretty much since it opened,'

'Good and how long is that?' I began to stutter at this point, I felt a bit like Hugh Grant.

'Six years now, I like it here. How about you? What do you do?'

'I used to be a financial advisor, but now I've come to London to become a writer.' We took turns in asking questions and really got to know each other. Then a small voice from the back of my head told me to ask her out on a date. I decided a rejection at this time would be idiotic and I was going to be living upstairs. After several glasses of orange juice, Kate returned to work and I waited for James to arrive.

I stared into the street and suddenly, like a ghost, Sean walks in. I stand in amazement, my subconscious goes into remission.

'Sean!' I called across the restaurant, 'Seany!' Then he walked over to me,

'You must be Vinny,' he said,

'Sean, stop messing around, what are you doing here?' He began to laugh,

'I'm not Sean…'

'But…

'I'm James. Sean is my twin brother,'

'But you look so alike,'

'I know, we used to get that a lot,' he kept smiling, 'It's good to finally meet you Vinny, sorry I was late, I had a few things to deal with,'

'No problem,' I looked in amazement,

'You hungry?'

'Yeah,' He looked over into the kitchen,

'Two tomato and mascarpone,' He shouted, 'I guarantee you, this is the best pasta sauce you'll ever taste, lets go and sit down,' I was still in shock. Their mannerisms were the same. James was wearing a black jacket that I was sure that Sean also owned. It felt slightly bizarre talking to a man crafted in Sean's image but not actually be Sean. I felt like I was talking to an amnesia sufferer.

We sat and I told him about Claire, Emily and my old job. We exchanged stories about Sean and ate a magnificent meal. We finished eating and I offered him a cigarette. Kate came over to collect the plates and she smiled at me.

'You better watch out for that one,' James remarked as Kate left,

'I'm sorry?' I pretended not to know what he insinuated,

'I saw that look,'

'What look?' I laughed

'The look, she's already taken. Sean told me to find you someone,'

'Thanks but I'm okay at the moment. I'm going to have to have a word with Sean,'

We laughed and drank; he told me about his life and about his girlfriend, Kelly. The restaurant became full and James insisted that I get some rest. I followed him through the hectic kitchen overflowing with smells of sun-dried tomatoes, Parmesan cheese and red wine. There were two men, one artistically cutting vegetables and the other mixing a pot whilst throwing in various different herbs. I followed James through a door, which led up to some stairs.

The apartment above was completely different to the restaurant below. Whilst downstairs was archaic and traditional, the upstairs was post modernistic. The first element to catch my eye was the Louis Armstrong poster that was framed in a glass case and hung near the fireplace. The large room consisted of a sitting area, dining area and a kitchen.

It was homely yet fashionable. The walls were dark blues and the whole flat was carpeted. James told me to make myself at home and so it was done. I sat on the brown leather settee and let out a sigh of relief. I switched on the television and rampantly flicked though the various channels. I was back into my perpetual bliss.

There were pictures on the mantelpiece of what appeared to be James with Kelly. I rummaged and found a picture of Sean and James together and I felt comforted that I was not clinically insane. I watched a sitcom or two and nodded off on a documentary about penguins. I dreamt of Claire and the wonderful Sundays we would spend together doing nothing. For the first time in a long time I felt comfortable, I had a lovely sofa and glorious television. What more could I need? Obviously, my old life would not go amiss and financial security would be nice.

I awoke with a mighty slam and stood before me was a woman. I tried to judge if it was yet another dream.

'Hi, you must be Vinny,' I was trying to figure out how everybody knew my name.

'Hello?' I muttered as the light blinded me,

'Sorry, did I wake you?'

'Don't worry about it,' I looked closely, 'I guess you are Kelly,'

'Yeah, can I get you a drink?'

'Um, just a glass of water please,'

'No problem,' she said in a very chirpy manner, 'So James says you've come here to make a fresh start?'

'Yeah, I had a few problems at home,'

'I'm sorry to hear that,' if you need anything, don't be afraid to ask,'

'Thank you,'

'No problem.' Kelly handed me a glass of water and smiled, 'You're going to be okay. Listen, get some sleep and I'm just going to help James downstairs. Come down if you need anything,'

'Thank you again,' as she left, I tried to relax. I could not get to sleep so instead I stared at the ceiling and contemplated my ideas. I thought about my book and how I was going to write it. I was throwing around a few ideas. I was thinking of something scary but most horror novels tend to be tugged and boring if written in the wrong way. I was not good enough to write something scary. I thought about writing a romantic comedy but the idea of writing something cliché and tacky did not appeal to me. I formed the notion of writing an autobiography but my life would probably seem uninteresting and I am not that vain.

I began to think about the autobiography and came to the realisation that it had been four months since I last had sex. I realised that I had sent myself into a destructive cycle and flicked on the television to stop myself from over thinking. A topless woman seducing a man was presented to me so I fumbled and changed the channel; again, I was presented by a provocative advert and every channel was the same. I switched off the television. I decided to go downstairs.

The stairs led into a pristine empty white kitchen, which I followed through into the dining area. I heard the sound of laughter; I entered into an empty restaurant and saw a group sitting around a table.

'Here he is,' came a reminiscent voice, 'come and join us, Vinny,' I walked over to see James, Kelly, Kate and the rest of the staff sitting around a table. 'I would like you to meet Kelly my girlfriend, Jake the head chef, Mark the second chef, Maria, Christina and Kate my waitresses,'

James had introduced everybody around the table. I shook hands and said hello.

'Do you feel a bit better?' asked Kelly,

'Yeah, great. I just needed to sleep off the jet lag.' I replied. They asked me questions about my old life and I took the time to get to know everybody around the table. We all got on really well. We laughed and talked. It felt good, I almost felt like a member of staff. We exchanged stories and I heard humorous nostalgic accounts of events that had happened in the restaurant.

Jake, the head chef, recounted a time when he got Mark, the second head chef to water the plants,

'And the plants were plastic!' We all laughed at the punch line.

'So, Vinny, we're a little understaffed and I need a new waiter. Would you like to join our motley crew?' asked James in a moment of seriousness.

'I would love to,' I replied,

'So it is, a toast to our new waiter and newest addition to the Little Italy family, Vinny,' we knocked our glasses together. Kelly mentioned something about calling in sick and it began a round of jokes and laughter. For two hours, I forgot about

Claire and Ireland. I was in London now and I had begun my new life. I promised myself I would call Emily in the morning and enjoyed the rest of my evening.

may

In the darkness came enlightenment. I gazed in wonder at the images presented to me in the glorious yet mysterious skies. I laid my body on the delicate forest bed and watched in awe. I created this. I am the first deity.

While lying in bed that gloomy London morning, I had become inspired. I wanted to write something original yet accessible. The idea was simple and came to me while watching a new Star Wars film. A prequel! Are you ready for this? A prequel to the BIBLE! Everybody loves prequels and the Holy Bible is one of the most read books in the world.

Smiling at my wonderful idea I asked James for directions to the nearest Waterstones and bought a copy of Paradise Lost by John Milton and a copy of the Holy Bible. I spent three days eating Italian food and skim reading the religious texts. The idea would be controversial at first but then you have to ask yourself, are not some of the most renowned and prominent works of literature in the twenty first century controversial? I could be the next Howard Marks.

The Holy Bible: A Prequel would obviously be a comedy and would show God as a small child. I am a genius! I began to ponder the implications and realised it would be a lot harder than I initially imagined.

As humans, we have no conception about what actually existed before the big bang. For all we know, there may have not been a big bang. There would not have been anybody around to hear it. I had free reign, I could create anything I wanted and there would be no one to contest it. I felt powerful.

God could have parents. He is one and so our creator would need a parental figure. The Holy Spirit would be the father of God and the Grandfather of Jesus. And of course, he would have his mother, nature.

I began to think of a setting for the novel. Heaven would not have been created yet so I would have to construct a new level; the time before time. It would make heaven look like a McDonalds. I was ready.

Before I decided to offend a whole religion, I thought it would be nice to see my parents. I had not seen my parents in well over a year, which fuelled the desire to pop in and say hello. I love my parents and we never had any major fights. We did, however, have the occasional shouting match. I always assumed that having a bad childhood was cool but to be honest, I had a good childhood. I am not ashamed to admit it.

My parents are a little unorthodox. My father was a stockbroker and my mother was a teacher. They live in Milton Keynes and have done for the best part of twenty years. I arrived at a Nandos Chicken restaurant down the road from Earls Court Underground station and consumed a lunch fit for a gladiator.

I arrived at Earls Court Station with a belly full of food and not a care in the world. This is until I entered the murky tubes of the underground in which I found to my dismay an enormous line for the ticket booths. I paid for my ticket and proceeded to an outdoor platform in which I waited with what seemed to be thousands of other Londoners.

I lit a cigarette and saw the train approach. I had to get to Victoria Station via the District line, which in turn would lead me to Victoria Station consequently leading me via the Victoria line to Kings Cross St Pancras. It seemed straightforward. I was a little confused but I had a map and so I could not falter.

To my dismay, I found I had taken the wrong train. I did what any rational person would do in my situation. I panicked. I was lost in wormholes and had no perception of where I was. I looked at the name of the line and found I had taken the District line to Edgware Road.

Edgware Road was empty. I found after smoking a packet of cigarettes and two minutes of ranting there was a train going to Kings Cross St Pancras by taking the Hammersmith and City line. Still with me? I arrived at Kings Cross St Pancras with a sense of accomplishment. I left the underground section and arrived at the main train station. I waited on the platform for the train to take me to Milton Keynes.

While sitting on the train I thought about my novel. Writing a prequel to the Holy Bible would be difficult because as far as most people believe, there was nothing. I wanted to give God a personality. I discarded the Mother Nature idea because it seemed too cliché.

I contemplated the various religious sects that would come after me. I concluded that most would have to forgive me. I decided that Lucifer would be God's younger brother and Heaven would eventually become a family business. I would end at the beginning of the Old Testament.

I arrived at Milton Keynes station and got into one of the many taxis that waited outside. I had to give the driver instructions to get to my parent's house. They live in a region of Milton Keynes called Shenley, which seems to be inhabited by the elderly.

I decided to surprise my parents because I could not conceive any other plan to explain that my wife had left me and had taken their only grandchild. I arrived at the old house like I had been away for five minutes. I rang the doorbell and my father answered,

'Vinny, you're home! Come in son,' he said cheerfully, 'Angela, your son is here!' as he said this, my mother walked out of the kitchen.

'Vinny, this is a surprise, come here and give your mother a hug,' she embraced me and while hugging asked, 'Where's Claire? And where is my beautiful granddaughter?'

'They couldn't make it,' I replied, 'I thought I'd come and visit you,'

'Come and sit down,' my father said. I think they knew what was happening at the time. My mother made tea and we had a lengthy conversation in which I told them what happened. We discussed my plans and I told them about the book. I realised that telling them what the novel was about would be too much for them.

'We're your parents and we want you to be happy…'

'…I didn't like that Claire girl,' my mother interrupted my father during his long-winded speech.

'We're your parents and we'll support any decision you make. How are you for money?'

'I'm okay, I think. I've got a job working at a friend's restaurant until I get myself sorted.' I paused, 'I still love her,' and then I cried. They both embraced me and it was a bonding moment. I cried like a child and eventually stopped when my dad made a joke.

I became nostalgic and went to my old room. My bed was made and the curtains were opened. I do not suppose my parents actually ever went into my room after I got married. I looked through some old photographs of some old friends and felt a calming reassurance. It felt good to be home and part of me did not want to leave.

I spent the entire weekend with my parents and found I had become a visitor. My mother fussed over me and father prescribed his thesis of the financial world and how my generation has over commercialised everything.

I drank copious amounts of tea and watched Countdown. The day eventually came when I had to leave them again and venture back into my new life. I gave them a number at which they could reach me. I now had to make the traumatic journey home.

The restaurant was split into two sections; the back of house which consisted of the kitchen and office and then the front of house which covered the dining area. I had to be trained on both. Kelly had bought me a white shirt and I already had trousers. James asked me to wear a half apron, which looked a little like a miniskirt.

My hair had grown longer than I usually allow it to. I stood posing in front of the long mirror in James and Kelly's bedroom. With my hair long, I appeared to be a little Italian. I tried out my Italian American accent,

'Are you talking to me? Are YOU talking to me? You gotta be talking to me because I'm the only one here...'

'Vinny? What are you doing?' Kelly interrupted me with a big smile on her face.

'Um... err... nothing, I was just...' I could not justify myself,

'James wants to teach you how we serve customers around here.' She said trying to hold back the raucous laughter. I took the little dignity I had left and went back downstairs.

'Hey Vinny, you and Kate have got the dining area tonight,'

'No problem,'

'Right, as a customer enters, you greet them at the door and show them to a table, non-smoking is the front of the restaurant and smoking is the back. Take the drinks and the starter orders and use what you need from the bar. The table numbers are written on the side of the tables. Write the order and table number and Kate will sort out the bill. It's pretty straightforward until you get busy.'

'No problem,' I lied. As he was speaking, I went into a little daydream about Kate. I missed everything but I had a vague idea.

The first set of customers entered and I watched Kate take the family of four (including the disgruntled teenage who really didn't want to be there) to their table. She took their drinks orders. She then took their starters and main order, and placed it in the hatch that led into the kitchen. It was like clockwork. She then began to re-stock the bar. I decided this would probably be the only time I would get to talk to her so I helped her by cleaning pint glasses.

'So how is your first night going so far?' She asked, every time she spoke I wanted to kiss her.

'A little daunting but you make it look easy,' I mumbled and probably offended her,

'Don't worry about it, you'll be fine,' and then she smiled, I knew then she was the one and I smiled back. James put on a classical Italian CD, which made anybody who came in feel as if they were in a film. I was having fun and in hindsight, I would rather do this than sit behind a computer all day.

I served a couple on their first date and made a couple of bad jokes but they were too nervous to notice. I served an office party who seemed not to actually be having a good time. It reminded me of my last job. At eleven, we became quiet but we had to remain open until twelve.

'Tough day?' Kate looked tired, I had an urge to hug her but I did not want to alarm her or for her to get the wrong idea about me.

'Yeah, I can't actually feel my feet anymore,' I replied,

'So, are you going to be in tomorrow?'

'I think so, I'm not sure,'

'Well if you're not, then who am I going to flirt with?'

'I, I, I, I, I…' I turned into Elmer Fudd,

'I'm just kidding, did you make any mistakes?'

'Not that I know of, well, except for the orange juice incident,'

'So how long are you going to be here?' I think she just wanted to make conversation so I kept it light.

'I don't know yet. As soon as my books published I guess,'

'You're writing a book?'

'Yeah, it's always been an ambition of mine,'

'Great. What's it about?'

'Um, it's…' I was not certain if I should tell her, 'it's a prequel,'

'Prequel? To what?'

'The Bible,' she fell about laughing after I said this, 'I'm being serious, it's what my book is about. I'm going to write about God as a little boy and eventually going to create the universe,'

'Oh my God,' she replied

'Exactly,'

'How much have you written?' she tried to compose herself as she questioned me,

'I haven't actually started yet, I'm getting around to it,' as I said this, a new set of diners entered the restaurant and we resumed our chores. As Kate took the time to get to know me, I thought I would question her. She talked for forty minutes about her boyfriend. Connor, her boyfriend, was in-between jobs and looking for something more professional. I did not ask what he used to do, I did not care. We closed up together and she called a taxi home. I went to see James in the office.

'Hey Vin, how's it going?' he seemed chirpy, we did well that night,

'Good, good,' I still felt a bit distant from James so I thought I would try to get to know him better. We talked for an hour about how he met Kelly, how they created the restaurant and a little about Kate. He only told me what I knew.

We had a beer and I told him about the book, he laughed. He told me I could borrow his electric typewriter but I needed to buy an ink cartridge. I decided to begin work that night.

James went to bed and I sat at the kitchen table with a pad of paper and a pen. I needed to write the first page to get an idea of how this was going to work. I yearned to create a sentence that everyone would remember.

I sat looking at this blank page. I put on some gentle music to inspire me but it was futile. I had writer's block and I had not even started yet. Then I had an epiphany.

Before there were stars and moons, before there were suns and planets there was a time before time. I had nothing, not even a soul. I am unique. I subsist in the forest of my father's imagination. I am Him.

I liked it, it was a little ambiguous but it worked; God as a child. It had not been tackled before and I think I understood why. I continued.

The rays of the sun crashed through the cracks of the canopy and onto the forest bed. I wandered through this lonely deep forest in search of raw preservation but found genuine passion. In the first time of my life, I had felt one with the organic trance of the forest.

The immersed brown of the forest bed merged with the lush greens of the trees. The scent of flowers surrounded me. The acres of dense woodland made me feel peaceful rather than alone. I sat quietly under an immense tree.

I was in absolute bliss. This rapture had become my seventh heaven. I rested until the sky grew dark. I began to appreciate every minute of life. This was beyond any Shangri-la. The trees towered over me like walls.

This was fantastic. I had my inspiration and I was away. Five minutes later, I reached a barrier. Again, I had given myself writer's block. I lit a cigarette and re-read what I had initially written. Just another sixty thousand words to go and at this point it seemed impossible. I began to daydream about things I cannot remember. My mind had hit a wall.

I made myself a cup of tea and stared at the few words I had written. I began to look around the kitchen and preoccupied myself by thinking about other things. I felt tired but I really wanted to get this over and done with.

I eventually concluded that if I had any likelihood of finishing this book I had to create a plan. Either that or I could undertake Virgil's theory and write a sentence a day but he died before he finished his book. Ten chapters each with six thousand words is my aim. I could easily write a thousand words a day because that would only be two pages. The only setback being able to fill two pages per day full of elevated diction and perfect syntax.

The first chapter would consist of God wandering in his father's forest. The second chapter would consist of Lucifer, the Holy Spirit, and their relationship with God. The third chapter would be God growing up and pronouncing his plans to create his own universe. After making a short plan for the first three chapters, I created a timetable for myself. One chapter per week, therefore I should finish by June.

'Still writing?' Kelly asked as she went to the kitchen to get a glass of water. She sat opposite me and lit a cigarette. 'How's it going?'

'Harder than I'd thought it would be,' I replied,

'Is this the prequel to the bible thing that you're writing?' I forgot that I told her.

'Yeah, I'm just getting a little stuck,'

'Don't worry about it, even the greatest writers must have got stuck from time to time?'

'Yeah, but not on the first page,'

'Okay, good point. I'm sure it'll all come to you,'

'Thanks,' I smiled.

'I'm going back to bed, night,' and she was gone. I resumed my mental trance and spent twenty minutes trying to get my pen to stand on end but to no avail. My mind became absent and I would try to do anything else other than write. I was waiting for an idea to come to me. I kept glancing at the kitchen clock but it would just become later and later.

I began to reflect on what I had written and considered if this was a good idea. I decided that my stamina would predominate and eventually retired to bed. I was happy with what I had written but I was still unsure how I would fill sixty thousand words. I had not exercised my mind creatively for a few years now and that night I slept like a baby.

I awoke the following morning well rested and looking forward to my next shift. I had left the first page on the kitchen table and saw James reading it,

'This is really good Vinny. Is the whole book going to be like this?' He seemed chirpy,

'I hope so,' I said in an enthusiastic tone,

'How long do you reckon it will take?'

'I reckon about three months before it's ready to proof read then I have to find a publisher,'

'Well, if I can help, just ask,'

'Thanks man,' I sat on the sofa and put on Saturday morning television.

'Scooby doo! I haven't watched that for years,' he said like a twelve-year-old,

'Yeah, Emily and I used to watch it all the time,'

'Of course, you have a daughter; I don't see you with a daughter,'

'Really?'

'Yeah, you look too young,'

'Thanks man,' I felt happy. We made jokes and reminisced about children's television of our day. I felt closer to James that morning and he seemed to resemble Sean in personality too.

We made breakfast together and watched more television. We spent an hour talking about music and we both like the same bands. It was almost like having Sean here with me. We talked more about the restaurant and my novel and connected on a deeper level. We had something in common, ambition.

Work that evening was difficult and very busy. I made mistakes but I managed to conceal them. I felt a bit depressed because we had many couples in that evening being a Saturday night. I did not get a chance to talk to Kate, but it felt good just having her in the same room. I could feel her positive energy all the way to table ten.

We all sat around drinking later that evening and exchanged a barrage of bad taste jokes. I sat with my orange juice and eventually joined in. I did not write that evening because I was too tired. Instead, I borrowed a CD from James and fell asleep to it.

june

I was peaceful in my father's sanctuary. In the time I had remained in His forest I had found enlightenment. It was time to create My own sanctuary. I could feel the crisp cool water on the soles of my feet and I walked across the great lake. I wandered towards the highest moon and eventually lead myself to the Kingdom of Light.

I woke with a notepad in my hand and still with no ideas. I had written the first chapter but I was still unsure about how I wanted the novel to progress. I decided to ring Emily and derive my inspiration from her. I sat on the sofa and I had the phone on my lap. I dialled the number and put the phone down. I realised then that she must hate me. What scared me the most was that she might not remember me.

I put the phone back on the table and collapsed back onto the sofa. I stared at the ceiling and thought about Emily. It will always be my duty to provide and love Emily. She would hate me if I stayed in Dublin and did not change. I would hate that too. I decided then to dedicate the book to her.

What if she did not remember me? What if she despised me? I began to panic. There was only one thing to do now; I had to go back to Dublin. I could get the rest of my things from Sean and more importantly, I could see Emily. I had a shower and got dressed. As I was leaving, I saw James and asked him if I could have a few days off.

James and I talked about money and I told him that I had enough saved up to survive for a while so he did not have to pay me a full wage. I said that I would work and contribute towards the rent and food. We were both happy with the situation and I was allowed to take days off from time to time. He told me there would be no problem and I went to Waterstones.

Walking through the streets of Earls Court, I realised the immensity of London. There were people walking everywhere and it made me feel rather insignificant. I walked from Trebovir Road past the underground station and to the Waterstones in Earls Court Road, which is opposite Barkston Gardens.

I picked up a Bill Bryson book because I needed a good laugh and I bought Emily a book about princesses. I started thinking about the cover of my book. I wanted something tasteful that would attract attention. My book is not farcical comedy but it is funny and purely fiction. I required the cover to display a similar sort of ambiguity but convey a sense of irony. 'The Holy Bible - A Prequel,' it had a nice ring to it.

I looked at different covers and I realised that I would have to write the book before I could think about the cover. I put thc Bryson back and paid for the book for Emily. I walked home that day with a new urgency, to write as if I had never written before. That night I began chapter two and did not rest until I had accomplished my two thousand words. After a six-hour writing bender, I binged on chocolate as my reward.

I typed up everything on James' typewriter and saw that I had been sitting for eight hours. I stood up to stretch and went for a walk. I knew of an all night internet coffee bar nearby and decided to stroll towards it. I got to the café at eleven that evening and spent over an hour and a half surfing the internet. I booked flight tickets to Dublin and enjoyed a large mocha. I felt contented; it was a good day.

The flight back to Dublin was less turbulent. I knew that I had Sean waiting for me and it felt like going home. I tried to sleep most of the journey but instead just rested my eyes waiting for the ordeal to be over.

I met Sean outside of the main terminal and he embraced me. I assume he did not realise he would miss me and part of me felt the same. We drove to his house and Michelle had made dinner. I gave Sean a tacky tee-shirt that I bought from a souvenir stall in Oxford Circus. After dinner, we talked about my new life in London and I told them about Kate. I mentioned the book but I needed an interruption before I resumed writing.

The following day I sorted a few things out at the bank and made certain I had enough money in my personal account. I then went to collect Emily from her grandmother's house. The taxi parked outside the house. I wanted to surprise her. I rang the doorbell and waited. Claire answered the door,

'Hi,' I said.

'Hi,' she replied. Then there was a very long pause. 'I thought you were in London, writing your book.'

'You heard about that?' I did not have anything to say to her, 'Is Emily with you?'

'Yeah, but she's asleep. Would you like to come in?'

'Yeah, that would be nice,' I entered her mother's house and it felt strange. It was like when we first met. We were civil to each other and she made some tea. We talked about everything except for what had happened to us then I brought it up,

'Why did you leave me?' I froze after I said this,

'I don't want to have this conversation Vinny.'

'Then what? You left and I'm the one who's suffering!'

'You don't understand, I have no idea where this new persona that you've created came from but I was bored, I needed something different,'

'I thought you loved me,' I tried to hold back the tears,

'I did, I do but it's not the same anymore,' she began to sob, 'I just can't be with you anymore,'

'Why didn't you tell me about him?'

'What has he got to do with anything?'

'HE RUINED MY LIFE!'

'YOU, YOU RUINED YOUR LIFE!' we were shouting like we always used to. I used to believe that couples that argued should break up but the arguments show passion. If two people did not care about each other, they would not argue. I care about Claire and always will. I would rather spend six hours arguing with her than a minute without her.

We sat on the sofa and both looked at the floor. She let out a sigh, looked at me, and said, 'I want a divorce,' she waited for my reaction. But I did not react; I stared at the floor not knowing what to say or what to do. It was a situation I could not deal with and I had no answers. We both heard Emily and she went to get her out of bed. Emily has to have a nap in the afternoons, otherwise she becomes grouchy.

'Can I have Emily for the day?' I asked her without even glancing at her.

'Sure, I'll get her things,' Claire replied and vanished into the bedroom. I looked up at Emily and opened my arms. She embraced me and suddenly I could breathe again.

'Where have you been?' She asked me,

'London,' I replied,

'With the Queen?' she asked

'Yeah, with the Queen. Emily, would you like to spend the day with me?' She nodded before I finished the sentence. I took a bag of Emily's things from Claire and left without saying goodbye. Emily waved goodbye for the both of us.

Using Sean's car I took Emily to McDonalds and we ordered more than we could eat. I gave her the book I had bought her and we sat on Sean's sofa and read it together. I convinced Sean to ring Claire and ask her if I could have Emily for the night and she could come and pick her up tomorrow.

Emily and I stayed up late and watched cartoons on the twenty-four hour cartoon channel and I put her to bed at eleven. Sean then got himself a can of beer and offered one to me.

'I still don't drink,' I replied.

'Really? You're doing well then,'

'Yeah, with everything that's happened, I don't really get the urge,'

'That's great, I'm proud of you,' he smiled as he said this, 'How's things with James?'

'Good, he's got a nice little company and a really nice girlfriend,'

'That's good to hear, I'll give him a ring tomorrow,' we talked until the small hours of the morning and laughed like we used to.

The following morning after a small cartoon session, Emily and I went to the park. We sat on the swings and I tried to explain to her what was happening between her mother and me. We talked about life and I told her I loved her and always would. We made each other laugh and I eventually took her home.

Claire arrived later that afternoon to collect her and we said our goodbyes. It never got easier, in fact each time I said goodbye to Emily, it hurt more. Sean and Michelle consoled me and later that evening, Sean dropped me off at the airport.

Sean parked the car but neither of us got out.

'When are you back next?' he asked,

'I don't know, I was thinking Christmas,'

'Okay, if you need to talk just phone me,'

'You too, buddy,' I opened the door, and got out, 'Why don't you and Michelle come and visit us?' I asked.

'I'll see what I can do,' He smiled,

'Thanks, Sean,'

'Anytime,' and with that he drove off. I walked to my terminal and headed back to London.

Back in London, I found myself unusually awake and inspired by my daughter I wrote more. I thought about Emily while I was writing. James and Kelly were giving me a lot of support and I actually felt like I was finally getting somewhere.

The light of the Venution moons crashed on my face in this mid summer bliss. This world I had landed on was seamless and unspoiled. The air was warm. I was comforted in thick green leaves. It was home. It was being a baby in a mother's womb. My insatiable need for thirst prevailed. I decided to wander the forest in exploration of water. I drifted through the immense plantation observing the peculiar creatures that inhabited this breathtaking planet. Creatures I could have never of fathomed. These gracious and forthcoming creatures did not appear ferocious but continued to subsist in the rapture of their planet.

I had never written anything so beautiful before. I had never tried but that is beside the point. I was pleased with my work. I lit a cigarette and continued to write. I created a story line. God is the son of the Holy Spirit. In Genesis and Paradise Lost, Lucifer is an angel. I wanted to have Lucifer as God's older brother. In my prequel, I will have Lucifer challenge his father because his father favours God. When God creates the heavens, I will have him create an arc angel in the likeness of his own brother in memory of him.

I was creating a complex story line with interesting characters. I wrote the story line in block form so I could make sense of it. I felt like a writer now, it felt good. I would finish my book where Genesis begun hence creating the perfect prequel.

Saturday night and we were under staffed. James was in the kitchen with the other chefs and Kelly, Kate and I were working the dining area. We had a hen night and a birthday party half an hour apart from each other. At ten o'clock, we ran out of most of our stock and so James went to Sainsburys to buy more ingredients. I was running around like a headless chicken.

I had three complaints, which I transferred to the kitchen staff. None of us that night had a break of any kind. There was a queue of customers out the door. We took nearly a grand that night. The midsummer heat made working harder. Just after eleven o'clock, I managed to spill soup on a customer but Kate told me not to give up. I apologised and Kelly gave them a free bottle of wine. I felt bad at the time but neither James nor Kelly seemed bothered in the least.

Kate was smiling throughout the whole of that shift. She kept on looking at me and I kept on looking at her. The heat subsided by midnight and James put on the fairy lights and the many candles that were scattered over the place. We killed the main lights and put on some soft romantic jazz music. At one o'clock, we stopped serving customers. The chefs cleaned what they could and went home leaving the four of us to tidy up. James and Kelly decided to go upstairs and celebrate their busiest day and told Kate and I to finish cleaning tomorrow.

I lit two cigarettes and gave one to Kate and we just sat in the midsummer heat. The last customers left two half bottles of wine so I cleaned some glasses.

'Are you okay?' Kate asked me,

'Yeah, I'm a little tired. How are you?'

'Good,' she pulled the hair band from her ponytail and her hair fell onto her shoulders. She ran her fingers through her hair and then poured us some wine. 'It's very romantic; the candles, the fairy lights, the wine, the music…'

'Yeah, I was just thinking about that,' I replied,

'How is your daughter?' she changed the subject, 'you took a few days off…'

'Yeah, great. It's just a little difficult her being so far away,'

'It must be tough, I couldn't imagine that,'

‘I’m coping, I ring her everyday and I’ll go and see her from time to time,’ I paused and there was a silence, we looked at each other and smiled.

‘So, how’s the book going?’

‘Good, good, I’m on chapter two at the moment,’

‘It seems like a difficult thing to write for your first novel,’

‘Yeah, I just really like the idea, it’s funny,’

‘How did you think up that idea?’

‘Well, my ex is a devout Catholic and I heard sections of the bible when she dragged me to mass every Sunday. I’ve been watching a lot of films recently and I’ve noticed prequels are a big thing at the moment so I combined the two ideas,’

‘I guess you’re not religious then,’

‘God no,’ She laughed as I said this. I love watching her laugh, ‘I just hope I don’t get in any trouble for writing it,’

‘I doubt you will,’ she was still smiling,

‘So how about you? What do you do when you’re not a waitress?’

‘I’m an artist; I paint and occasionally sculpt,’

‘Fantastic. You know, I’m looking for someone to do the cover of my book,’ I have no conception of what I just said. I have just asked her to design the cover of my book and I do not even have a publisher. I asked her this because she was a pretty girl.

'Really? That would be great; I'd love to do something like that,'

'It's settled. You are now my official cover designer,' I raised my glass and she subsequently raised hers. 'To us!'

'To us,' she remarked as we tapped glasses and drank. I have already proposed an idea that I may not be able to deliver so, being half man and half idiot, I decided to ask her about her boyfriend,

'So James tells me you have a boyfriend,' what am I doing?

'Yeah, kind of, well-ish,'

'Ish?'

'We're not, what you may call, conventional. We're very on and off and he keeps on cheating on me,'

'And you put up with this?'

'I've never really been able to prove him wrong and he manages to turn everything around,'

‘Sounds like a nice guy,’ I blurted this out realising that I cannot really pull off sarcasm.

‘He is. Well, he can be… sometimes,’ she stopped smiling; ‘can we talk about something else?’

‘Yeah, of course,’ and we did. We talked about everything until four in the morning when I walked her home. Chelsea is very quiet at half past four on Sunday mornings so we had the city to ourselves. We held hands and made each other laugh. It was the best hour of my life. I walked her home and we stood outside. I looked at her in the morning light and felt my knees weaken.

I wanted her to invite me in but I knew she would not. We were both a little drunk and very tired. She kissed me on the cheek and went in. I stood there. I could not move. I closed my eyes and relished in this perfect moment. I eventually walked back to the restaurant and went to bed.

I dreamt about her that night. I then thought about Claire and how I once felt the same way about her. I missed Claire and part of me was still in love with her. I convinced myself that I was not in love with Kate and it was just a crush. It would not be fair because she was in a relationship albeit a dysfunctional one but nonetheless a relationship and I was on the rebound. I had to recover from my last relationship before I began a new one.

James woke me the following morning and we cleared up the restaurant. I told him about the night before and he told me that I made the right decision. It took us two hours on that Sunday afternoon to clean the restaurant.

'So you drank?' James asked,

'Yeah,' I remembered it then, 'I don't know, I haven't drunk since I moved here. I just went with the moment,'

'You don't seem to just go with the moment often then?'

'Being with her is different, I become a different person and I like it. I spend most of my time worrying… but when I'm with her I gain in confidence,'

'Sounds like you're falling for her,' James laughed,

'Yeah, I guess so,'

'So you're not an alcoholic?'

'I don't think so.'

'Do you want a drink now?'

'No, I presume it was because I was in a bad place and I don't need it anymore,'

'I'm glad you came here Vinny, you're a good guy.'

'Thank you,'

'But a bad waiter.' I laughed as he said this, 'you are getting better, though.'

'I'll try harder.' We left the clean restaurant that afternoon ready to open up later that evening. James had to go and see his accountant, I had a little nap.

That evening we were not as busy. By ten o'clock, we only had three tables full so James asked us to do a spring-clean. I was asked to water the plants and was given a watering can. After five minutes of watering the plants, I heard raucous laughter coming from the kitchen. I walked into the kitchen to investigate and found that everybody on shift was in the kitchen laughing.

'What's so funny?' I asked,

'The plants…' the laughing stopped Kelly from finishing her sentence, '…are plastic!' and the laughter became thunderous. Part of me felt like an idiot but the other half felt accepted. I had become one of them now. I began to laugh.

‘I’m sorry, we do that to everyone when they start,’ James chuckled as he spoke, ‘you’re the first person to actually do it,’ we all laughed and eventually we all got back to work. After the watering incident, I became more relaxed at work and started to become a good waiter.

july

The waves of Chaos seemed to continue forever. Frenzied winds blew forcefully on my return to the first universe. I stretched my arms wide open as I glided into my chosen portal. My father's favourite kingdom was in-between twelve beautiful galaxies that surrounded his beloved sanctuary. From here, he controlled existence. This is my home.

The heat of summer made Little Italy unbearably hot, on the other hand, Kate arrived at work with a very sexy thin white shirt. Tables became full of tourists wanting to savour the taste of authentic Italian food during their stay in London. We even had a few Italians dining with us on a regular basis. They had flown thousands of miles from a beautiful hot country to eat pasta in London.

I even learned a little Italian from Cristina, one of the waitresses, in addition to my new Italian friends who could speak only a little English. James was in his element and because of the sudden rush of customers; we found a regular occurrence of tips and bonuses.

Of the hundred pounds I made per week, I gave James fifty-five and sent Emily fifteen leaving me thirty pounds a week. I did not mind giving James over half my wages because renting a place in London would be far more expensive and at least this way I get food included.

Kelly had bought me a new uniform for the summer months and I became constantly paranoid that people could see my nipples through my shirt. When this is your biggest problem in life, you know things are going your way. My hair had begun to cover my ears and had never been this long. I played with my hair a little more than I used to.

Today was no exception, it was exceptionally warm and the heat wave had given me a slight tan. I stood in front of the mirror trying to convince myself that I looked like Antonio Banderas. I took five orders in the first hour and did my usual small talk with the customers. I made the same jokes and offered the same specials. It was a good day.

At seven o'clock, we had a queue and again I found we were under-staffed. I tried to communicate with a German family but somehow managed to insult them and they soon left. I had customers shouting at me in at least twelve different languages and began to differentiate between the customers by accent rather than table numbers.

I had complaints ranging from cold food to something that was spelt wrongly on the menu. My paradise had become hell. Kate somehow seemed to be having fun and I found myself staring at her. The problem with this would be that I was ignoring customers while they were shouting at me and therefore made them even angrier.

We took more that night than ever before. I almost quit three times because of the pressure but every time I took off my apron, Kate would smile at me. When I was thinking of her I did not realise I was working, thinking, or breathing. She hypnotised me.

That night Kate and I stayed to clear up due to the fact that James promised us twenty pounds. We knew we could do it in an hour and so twenty pounds in one hour seemed reasonable.

We rushed everything and the kitchen was tidy so we finished early. I asked Kate if she wanted to share a bottle of wine with me and after considerable deliberation, she finally caved in.

'So did you always want to be a writer?' She asked.

'Yeah, I did a degree in finance because there was more money in it,'

'I understand, I always wanted to be an artist,'

'Really? What sort of art?' I asked,

'Abstract, I love how shapes and colours can convey a message,'

'You should do that you know,'

'No, I don't have the time and the course I want to do is too expensive,'

'Where is it?'

'Saint Martin's College of Art and Design, it's in Islington. I wanted to do a portfolio course but I haven't had the time,' we talked about the restaurant and I told her a bit about my old job. We laughed about the Italian family and how they could be linked to the mafia.

'What's you favourite Mafia film?' She asked me,

'Well, everyone is going to say the Godfather…

'…with the exception of the Godfather,'

'Um… Goodfellas. You?'

'Analyze this,' she replied,

'That's not a mafia film!' I laughed, 'It's a crappy Billy Crystal film,'

'It had the mafia in it, I liked it,'

'But it's not a mafia film,' I protested,

'But I think De Niro is hot,' she smiled as she exclaimed this,

'I prefer Pacino; he's a better actor,'

'I don't think I've seen any other Pacino films,'

'What about Scent of a Woman?

'Oh, I liked that,' she kept smiling and then she announced 'I prefer Brad Pitt films,'

'I'm guessing it's not because of his skills as an actor,'

'He was so hot in Fight Club,' she paused, 'So what actresses do you find sexy?'

'Cameron Diaz but I think every man would agree with me. I find actresses intimidating; I wouldn't want to date an actress,'

'Did you see her that film she did with Tom Cruise?'

'Vanilla Sky? Yeah it was a good film, it really made me think. I liked the idea…' and then she kissed me. She cut me off mid sentence and just kissed me and kept on kissing me. It was an amazing kiss until she pulled away. I however stayed where I was with my eyes closed until I heard her laughing.

'This has been fun, Vinny,' she said while blushing a little, 'I have to go,'

'Yeah, I…'

'I'll see you tomorrow,' she said as she left and I stood there transfixed at the door trying to comprehend the action that just took place. I thought she would say something; like profess her undying love for me or apologise for accidentally thinking I was someone else.

I lay in bed that night pondering the outcome of this situation. Do I confront her with the situation or declare my love to her? Should I stay quiet and hope that she makes the next move? She has a boyfriend; will he thrash me? All these questions kept me up for most of the night.

I watched the moonlight shoot through my bedroom window and hoped for some sort of understanding. After a plethora of deep thoughts, I think I figured out what women want. I know this question has been asked for thousands of years but on that eventful evening, I figured it out. The thing that women want is what they cannot have. Women want what they cannot have, of course, it makes sense. I have answered a question that theologians have been pondering for years!

When I was working as a financial advisor, there was a woman in the office that was constantly hitting on me. I now knew why, she knew I was married and therefore knew she could not have me. Women always go for the man who does not want to be in a relationship while the men running around acting desperate are not getting a thing. I should write a book on this.

The next day I spent a few minutes marvelling at my genius and set about to write chapter three of my book. I began to criticise myself as a writer and concentrated on the way I was writing. The words I used and the way my sentences were forming appeared to become more colloquial. I needed to get on with the story line and focus less on the imagery.

I wanted to give God human characteristics but innocent and childlike. I did not want to attempt to give much attention to the Holy Spirit because that would spark more questions. I wanted to explain the bit before the bible in a creative manner.

For two and a half-hours a day, I would spend gazing into blank pages without writing a word. I churned out on average about five hundred words a day but that does not exclude the weeks that I left the writing to concentrate on other things. When I wrote I would become increasingly tired and start misspelling some words. I would look over to the sofa and will myself to continue writing.

I stumbled upon a great waterfall; the forest succumbed to an oasis of tremendous beauty. This splendour eclipsed the rays of the various suns. I was blinded by the magnificence of this streaming cascade. I was lured by a thirst. I cupped my hand and drank the shimmering clear water. My thirst had been quenched.

I read over what I had written and found I had still not mentioned that this character was in fact the son of the Holy Spirit and the father of the Holy Son. It was at that moment I began to type without thinking and just began to write.

In the darkness came enlightenment. I gazed in wonder at the images presented to me in the glorious yet mysterious skies. I laid my body on the delicate forest bed and watched in awe. I created this. I am the first deity.

I decided on whom I would want to play God if this book is ever made into a film. As long as it was not Leonardo DiCaprio, I had no reservations. I wanted to finish Chapter three as soon as possible because I knew that Sean's wedding was approaching and I knew it would disrupt my deadline.

After another two hours with nothing to show, I decided to take a walk and find some inspiration. I slipped on my trainers and after a frantic search for my keys; I wandered into the outside world. The midsummer evening made the streets glow gold from the sun. I decided to follow the sun and kept walking until my surroundings became unfamiliar.

I walked past a yoga class and a busy trendy London restaurant. People were living their lives and it just seemed to work. Life is what you make of it and I realised then the beauty of life. I am fortunate to be living in a first world country and I have the ability to achieve my ambitions. This was not enough inspiration; with every step, I had more thoughts and more ideas.

Eventually I discovered a small church and saw the doors open. I wandered in and instantly fell in astonishment in the sheer beauty of this construction. I sat on a pew and listened to what seemed to be the angels singing. I looked up at a window and gazed as the sun broke through and illuminated the statue of Mary.

I do not believe in God. I do not think than God created man but man created God in his own subconscious. I read about an experiment that had a hundred people standing in a circle holding hands and concentrating on lighting a bulb. As humans, we only use ten percent of our minds leaving ninety percent free for the subconscious. If enough people believe in something then the ninety- percent will create it. Our own existence could be the result and the cause of a great paradox. What came first, the God or the belief?

I thought about what I wanted my book to say. Rather than just aggravate a whole religion I wanted to send a message that people would think about. I sat quietly with my thoughts and thought about Emily and Claire. I had a lot to think about and I need sleep. I put some change in the collection box and returned home.

I wrote more rapidly than I had before. My fingers were aching and my mind became absent but I did not relent. I wrote without thinking and spelt every other word wrong. I made no difference, I was writing and I could always salvage what I liked from this mess of ideas and descriptions.

Little Italy had calmed a little and it became bearable to work there again. I enjoyed working with Kate and asked Kelly to switch all our shifts so we were constantly working together. Kate never mentioned our kiss and things felt how they were before. Something had changed between us though but for some reason we managed to hide it.

The summer months meant that we would usually spend the day together in the park or walk through the city centre. We spent a lot of time together but the one element I kept forgetting was her boyfriend. She would mention him from time to time but we never conversed about him.

The heat soared during the last week of July and this made working in a restaurant difficult. James had been negotiating with the air conditioning companies but they were all over charging. Kate was in her stunning white shirt and I became even more paranoid that the customers were laughing because they could see my nipples through my white shirt.

Kate asked if she could finish early that night but I never found out why. At eight o'clock, a large thug entered the restaurant. I looked at him and my knees began to give way. For a moment I thought that this beast was going to kill me and everyone else in the room until I realised who he was. Kate embraced the large man and kissed him on the cheek. Kate and the creature came over to me and Kate introduced him to me.

‘Vinny, this is Connor, Connor this is Vinny,’ she said smiling,

‘Good to meet you, mate,’ he growled in a Barry White style voice. At first, I did not understand what he said; his voice was so deep that only crabs at the bottom of the ocean could understand what he was saying. He must know that Kate and I have been spending a lot of time together and I did not want to be killed by this monster of a man so I put on a camp voice and gave every impression I was gay.

Kate and her primate boyfriend left the restaurant. I think he took her to the top of the Empire State building. James came over to me and asked me why I was trembling. I ignored him and continued to work.

After a long and tiring day and my confrontation with the Nutty Professor’s older and larger brother I felt tired. James and I were on the rota to clear up and I thought this would be the perfect opportunity to ask why Kate was dating a professional wrestling reject.

‘So what do you think of him?’ James asked,

'I think it's funny how, as we speak, there is a team of Japanese scientists trying to figure out on how to destroy that thing,' I replied.

'I meant Connor,'

'So did I,'

'Someone jealous?' he teased.

'No, someone shit scared,' I decided talking to James was like being in secondary school again and no one wants to face that trauma. Nevertheless, curiosity got the better of me and the line of questions began.

'So how did they meet?' I asked in a concerned friend kind of way.

'He pretty much saved her life.' James paused to make sure he had my attention, 'Kate and the others used to go clubbing every Friday night and one night some crazed girl tried to stab Kate with a broken glass bottle. Connor stopped the fight and got injured in the process.'

'Why did this girl attack Kate?' I asked,

'Kate started to date her ex-boyfriend and crazy girl didn't have any closure. She blamed Kate for the break up of her relationship.'

‘How long have they been seeing each other?’ I had a question ready before he even finished answering the last one.

‘About six months now. They seem to be getting on well but none of us really know Connor,’

‘So he’s a bodyguard?’

‘Yeah,’ James stopped mopping as he said this and looked me straight in the eye, ‘Look Vinny, I think you’re a good guy and to be honest I don’t think much of this Connor bloke but the thing is you’re still married albeit separated but you need to sort yourself out first. I would advise not getting into another relationship while you’re in your situation especially with someone who is already in a relationship,’ James continued to mop the floor.

‘I kissed her,’ James stopped and looked at me in disbelief. ‘Well, she kissed me and I didn’t stop her, it was a mutual thing…’ there was a pause,

‘How was it?’ He asked,

‘Good, good. I…’

‘Be careful, Vinny; try not to make things too complicated.’ James put the mop back into the bucket and grabbed his coat, ‘I’m in the mood for coffee, want to join me?’

'Sure,' I replied while putting the cleaning cloths in the bin. We drank coffee and talked about my situation. We talked about Sean and his marriage to Michelle. James told me that he booked tickets for us so we could attend the wedding. He told me of his conversation with his brother. He explained how Sean feels a bit lonely without me.

I missed Sean too and was very much looking forward to his wedding day. James gave me a lot of advice that morning. We discussed mafia films and why Pacino is a better gangster than De Niro and we went home as the sun was rising.

august

From the forest of knowledge of good and evil, I recovered a single tree. I admired the beauty of the tree and left it in my father's sanctuary. I wandered the theological pastures looking for my beloved father, the Holy Spirit.

I let James sit adjacent to the window after he put me under the impression that he rarely flew. I was contemplating the situation of having Sean and James together in a room and the confusion. Their dress sense was similar which was going to make things even more difficult so I suggested they wear name labels.

'That would take the fun out of it,' he replied in a mock Irish accent,

'I suppose you're right. By the way, try the Guinness in Ireland,'

'Why?'

'Just trust me, it tastes completely different, it's like the best alcoholic drink you can have for breakfast,'

'I'll take your word for it,' James unbuckled himself at least ten minutes after everyone else did, 'Is Claire going to be there?'

'Probably, I haven't given it much thought,' I replied,

'Do you reckon it'll be awkward?'

'I'm not sure, if she brings Rob then I'll have to deal with it and if she doesn't then I don't see a problem,'

'How is this going to work though? You're Sean's best man and she's Michelle's maid of honour…'

'How do you know all this?'

'I talked to my brother last night; he told me what was happening,'

'I don't know. It hasn't really registered that she is going to be there. I haven't thought about the inevitable fact that she might bring him. At the moment, Claire is no longer a person. When I see her I won't be meeting my soon-to-be ex-wife, I will be looking at six months of heartbreak and depression. The only thing that scares me now is that it might all come flooding back and I do not want that. I want to move on. On the bright side, I will get to see my daughter. Emily is my light, she is my legacy and the last thing I want is for her to be exposed to this. Deep down I know that if Claire and I get back together, things will never go back to how they were and she will have a set of parents who are constantly wondering if they should be together.'

'I've got a funny feeling this weekend is going to be a lot harder than I first thought. On a lighter note, do we get lunch on this flight?' James responded, he understood what I was feeling and tried to change the subject.

'I think so; I don't eat on planes,' we eventually received our lunch and I gave mine to James. Ironically, they served us this small pasta salad and James gave me another lecture on Italian food. For the first time in my entire life, I landed at the right time and we headed straight for the main terminal to meet with Sean and Emily.

Emily ran up to me and gave me a hug as I lifted her. She looked at James in a confused manner and

I explained to her that James is Sean's identical twin brother. She looked at Sean and started laughing. I laughed with her.

Sean embraced his brother and the similarity was remarkable. When compared, the two had the same mannerisms and almost the same voice. I remembered what they were wearing so I could differentiate between the two.

Emily did not release me from her loving grip until we got into Sean's car. She could not get over the fact that Sean had a twin brother. I became nostalgic as we drove through the streets of Dublin. My old life seemed like it ended long ago and part of me felt like I had returned home. We arrived at Sean's house and Emily told me she was staying the night with Sean and me because her mother and Kelly had things to sort out for the wedding.

Emily's birthday was the next day and I bought her a Barbie playhouse and plenty of little accessories that Kate helped me pick out. She understood what was going on between her mother and I and she was very brave about the whole affair. I was going to take her out for the day but that night after a couple hours of cartoons I had to talk to Sean and James and figure out how I was going to survive the wedding.

'Their having problems already,' Sean announced while he got himself and James a beer. I told him that I would not drink during the course of my stay because it would lead to problems. It gave me the opportunity to be the designated driver on the night and Sean said he would let me drive his car.

'What problems?' I asked,

'She's moved back in with her mother and seems to be there every day. The last time I saw her was when she came over and burst into tears,' He said this as if it had no consequence at all. He may have thought I was over her. To be honest, I may I have thought I was over her. It was clear that I was not and James picked up on this but remained silent. I could not decide if I was happy or sad.

'Will he be there at the wedding?' I asked,

'Probably not,' Sean replied. I felt like dancing. This was great. I had some hope. We talked about what I was going to do and I informed Sean about my dysfunctional and somewhat non-existent relationship with Kate. The strange thing about the whole situation was that when I was in London, all I could think about was Kate but now I am in Dublin, the only person that matters is Claire.

We spent the evening talking about the wedding and how our lives had taken an unexpected turn. I felt like I was part of that family and kept on referring to myself as the good-looking brother.

Emily woke me up on that glorious summer morning. We began with a hearty breakfast in McDonalds and followed it by going to the Dublin Zoo. The Dublin Zoo is split into four sections and Emily loved to go to the blue section where all the monkeys are. We spent the day giggling at the chimps and Emily reminded me constantly that I look like a gorilla.

We took a taxi from the zoo and we went to see a Disney film at the cinema. The film had a moral story and a funny character. It was like every other Disney film but the idea worked.

After the cinema, we set off back to Sean's house where Emily opened her presents and ate the pizza we ordered. We watched television and I put her to bed. Sean had taken James on a sight seeing tour, which meant a tour of every pub in Temple Bar.

When Sean and James returned, James and I went about planning Sean's stag night.

The next day Claire dropped off Michelle and picked up Emily while I was still asleep. Emily had taken all her clothes and toys with her. This eradicated all the mess from Sean's living room. James made breakfast for Sean and I and we all went to hire tuxedoes. James also bought an awful second hand wedding dress so when we got Sean utterly drunk he would wake up as the bride.

We bought copious amounts of alcohol from Sainsburys and the rest of Sean's friends began to turn up. The twelve of us went to the Mexican restaurant that Sean and I used to visit regularly. Each of us bought Sean a cocktail before the food even arrived and he was drunk before we began dessert. We stole a sombrero from the restaurant and affixed it to the drunken groom.

We went to a bar and Sean was force-fed eleven pints of Guinness. James also drank Guinness that evening, and in fact did find it to be the best alcoholic drink in world, and indeed confirmed that there was no comparison to the appalling black water that we are served in the rest of the United Kingdom.

One of Sean's work friends suggested that we go to a strip club and as none of us had any objections whatsoever we marched onward to the nearest strip club we could find. We left the restaurant devastated and we all chipped in to pay the obscenely high bill. Sean on the other hand was in submission and just wanted to go home.

We stumbled upon a large building with a dark exterior and neon lights. We entered and ordered more drinks. Sean ordered an orange juice but in return got a bottle of champagne. We watched the beautifully curvaceous woman parading on a small metal stage. Most men do not find strip clubs erotic and find the beautiful women intimidating. Sean was too drunk to focus properly and so did not fully appreciate the surroundings.

James paid for Sean to have a private lap dance, which rendered him semi-conscious. At two o'clock in the morning, we left in search of food and found ourselves in a kebab shop. Sean had passed out in the back of his own car and so James thought this would be the perfect opportunity to strip him and put on the wedding dress. We decided not to tie him to a lamp-post because Dublin is a dangerous city and one of his workmates mentioned how sexy he would look in a wedding dress.

A random girl in the kebab takeaway offered to do his makeup and afterwards he looked like a guest on the Jerry Springer show. We took him home and took pictures of him from various angles. It was a cruel thing to do but we found it hilarious.

We quietly put him to bed and tried not to wake Michelle. The idea of Michelle seeing her future husband in a wedding dress on their wedding day just seemed too funny not to attempt. James and I contemplated on what we should do with the pictures and decided to keep them and use them for blackmail later. We could not stop laughing about Michelle's reaction in the morning and eventually nodded off to sleep.

The next morning we awoke to the terrified scream of a woman. James and I, half-asleep ran into Sean's bedroom and were promptly chased out by Michelle. We stood in the kitchen unable to stop laughing. Michelle screamed at us and finally started laughing with us and we showed her the pictures. She eventually saw the funny side of it. James made breakfast and we sat at the kitchen table.

'You bastards!' A voice came from the bedroom, 'Bastards! Bastards! Bastards!' We began to laugh again and then when Sean finally walked into the kitchen we erupted into rapturous applause. Sean looked angrily and James and I and went back into the bathroom.

Sean soon forgave us and we got ready for the wedding. Sean gave me the rings and he and James went to greet his family. It was a secular wedding because neither Sean nor Michelle were very religious. The registry office was very dull and it gave the wedding a low-key feel. Michelle looked beautiful and the fact that she was pregnant gave her a further glow. It was very tasteful and they hired out a bar for afterwards.

The ceremony began with Emily throwing rose petals behind the happy couple and then followed by Claire, myself, then Michelle's younger sister and James. This was the first time I had seen Claire since I had returned and ironically, we were walking down the aisle.

The ceremony began conventionally but then the couples read their own vows. Michelle turned to Sean and looked him in the eyes,

'You give me faith and devotion,
I now believe in dreams that come true,
My heart skips a beat every time you are near,
I know I will always be there for you.
You are the best thing in my life,
I miss you when you are gone,
You put me in a daydream trance,
When I run my fingers through your hair,
Your intense eyes are a window to your soul,
Being with you is all I care.' At which point Michelle's mother cried like a mountain dog. Then Sean turned to Michelle and with a tear in his eye recited his vows,

'Your smile would sink a thousand ships,
It would make a grown man fall to his knees,
It makes me realise how much I need you,
For you I would swim the seven seas.
To have known you is exceptional,
To have you a part of my world,

To feel this passion for you,
When I think of you, I become me again.
You are my world, my thoughts, my life,
I spend every minute thinking of you,
You are an inspiration to everyone you meet,
I want to spend every minute with you.
You're my angel, my one and only,
To me, you are the one.' At which point even James and I were sobbing even though we helped him write it. The newlyweds kissed and ran down the aisle. The entire congregation met in the pub afterwards and we drank ourselves silly. Everyone took it in turns to congratulate the happy couple and the children played happily in the corner.

The pub was decorated in a very Irish manner. There were old Guinness adverts pasted on the walls and a wall of bottled Irish spirits behind the ancient wooden counter.

James developed his Irish accent and convinced at least three people he was an Irishman. A few of the men that were involved in the previous night's celebration of bachelorhood came to congratulate James and me.

The time came when I had to make my best man speech. I stood on a chair while the landlord unplugged the jukebox. I tapped on the champagne glass and asked for everyone's attention.

'I would just like to say a few words in honour to the bride and groom. Today my friend Sean got married to a beautiful woman. The same man who looked like his beautiful bride last night.' At which point all the men in the room laughed while all the women stood silent, 'Joking aside, Sean has been a pillar to me and I know he will make a good husband. Michelle is like the older sister I never wanted and it's good to see two friends happy and in love.' I raised my glass, 'To being happy and in love,' at which point Claire rushed out of the room.

I decided not to follow her and left things as they were. Sean and Michelle left for their honeymoon in Paris and James and I made our way to the airport. It was one of the most stressful weekends of my life. I said my goodbyes to Emily, which she had become accustomed to. I promised to ring her the following day; a promise which I never broke.

On the plane, James and I talked about marriage and the possibility of reconciliation between Claire and myself. I liked my new life and valued my independence. We returned home and James gave a detailed account of what had happened during that illustrious weekend.

The restaurant was still busy and we finally changed our specials, which confused everyone. Kate seemed more distant and I kept thinking about Claire. What if I followed her? What if I begged her to come back to me? My mind was crammed with what-ifs?

I on the other hand began to write. Seeing Claire had given me inspiration. When I finish this book, it will prove to her and in some respects, myself, that I do not need her in my life and I can be successful and fall in love. And so, chapter four began with some of my best writing. I spent at least six hours a day writing and re-writing. I felt more awake than I have ever felt.

september

My father revealed to my brother, Lucifer and I, plans to create a new heaven and his new servants, which he named angels. We admired the sheer splendour of his vision and I began to worship him. I presented my father with the tree I had brought him and we shared an enlightened moment.

It was still very warm for mid September and I was grateful for the Indian summer. Little Italy was becoming less busy giving me time during my shift to let my mind wander. My birthday was coming up soon and this would be my first birthday in a long time without Claire.

I thought about Claire everyday and rang Emily more than I used to. Sean rang and told me she moved back in with her mother. I felt victorious; as if I had won a battle but proved to be a victory won at too great a loss. I had not written for days, which made me feel more insignificant in this monstrous metropolis.

I realised then what was bothering me. I am going to be twenty-seven years old. Twenty-seven may not seem like much but if you put it into context, it made me feel old. When my father was twenty-seven, he had a five-year-old son, a happy marriage and his own business, house and car. I have stains on my shirt.

Age is a tricky subject and the idiots that walk around saying things like 'You're as old as you feel' make it worse. The truth is you are as old as you are but it should not affect how you feel. Most teenagers between twelve and sixteen want to be eighteen. Most eighteen-year-olds want to be in their early twenties. Most twenty-year-olds want to be eighteen again. People who are forty kid themselves and pretend life is just beginning.

The truth is we all want to be in our mid twenties. The sitcom Friends is not aimed at people in their early twenties but for people who want to be in their mid twenties. These people actually tend to be between the ages of fourteen and forty. The other element of being twenty-seven is that I was going to be thirty soon. Most people want to be free and single but not at the age of forty. I have achieved nothing extraordinary.

On the day of my birthday, I woke with the sound of my alarm clock. I spent the day writing and found myself alone in the apartment in the early evening. Emily rang me in the morning to wish me a happy birthday. We talked for about half an hour until her grandmother told her to get ready for school.

Kelly came upstairs to see if I was okay and asked me if I was hungry. She asked me if I wanted to join James and her for dinner. We rarely ate together but the last couple of weeks have been dead allowing us to spend the shifts sitting down and talking.

'I'll be down in a minute, I've just got to finish this off,' I replied,

'No problem,' Kelly spoke as she walked into her bedroom. I packed up my notes in a folder and quickly brushed my hair. I washed my face in cold water and walked downstairs.

'SURPRISE!' I was at the receiving end of a thunderous roar. I entered the room slightly shocked.

I smiled for the first time that day as I walked through the room filled with new friends and customers who had become friends.

Kate stood in the middle of this and was one of the firsts to come and give me a kiss. After I received an entourage of kisses and well wishes, James gave me a big comedy kiss. Cristina brought out a birthday cake with twenty-seven candles on it.

'You know when you're getting old when you get a suntan off your birthday cake,' James announced. Everyone laughed and I prayed I would not get the birthday bumps. James presented me with a large wrapped present.

'We all chipped in together,' James said,

'You shouldn't have,' I felt a little guilty because these people had taken me into their lives. I opened the wrapper and found a plain cardboard box. Inside the cardboard box was a laptop computer.

'We figured that you would need something like this to get your work done more efficiently,' Kelly said. I gave Kelly and James a hug and thanked everyone. We opened bottles of wine and I opened some birthday cards. I even got a birthday card from my Italian friends.

The lack of customers meant we could close early and continue having the party. More people turned up and it became more of a post-summer staff party. Near the end of the evening, most of the guests left and the rest of us drank ourselves silly. I drank that evening but not excessively. I had less than a bottle of wine but because I did not drink much, I found the alcohol had more effect on me.

We sat around a large round table and talked about music and books. This was the first time since I moved in that everyone was together. We took turns in making bad jokes and laughed at each other's anecdotes. Around midnight people started to leave until it was only James and I left.

'Did you have a good birthday?' James asked.

'Yes. Thank you, I needed this,' I replied gratefully,

'No problem, you've seemed a bit down since we got back from Dublin. What's wrong?'

'Nothing,' I paused realising that he would not let this go until I told him how I felt, 'I miss Claire. I hear songs that remind me of her. When I walk through the city, part of me is looking for her,' I could tell I had his full attention. 'I just can't stop thinking about her. You know that feeling in the pit of your stomach that you can't get rid of? I'm feeling stage two in its full painful glory,'

'Stage two?' James questioned,

'People go through three stages during a break up; denial, depression and acceptance. I'm still in stage two and it hurts like crazy,'

'What are you going to do?'

'I don't know. I have thought about it but there is nothing I can do. I miss her. The worst bit of it all is when I wake up, I have woken up next to her every morning and when I reach over to her I find she is not there.'

'I'm not going to give you any advice because my advice will come from my own nostalgia while what you're experiencing is a matter of the proverbial heart,'

'Thank you, James. You are a good friend. This is something I have to deal with on my own. I think that's one of the reasons I'm writing this book, I need some sort of closure. Most days I just want to stay in bed and not move. My self esteem is shot and I don't feel like myself.' James just sat there as I attempted to explain how I felt.

'Throughout our whole relationship, I wanted to be the hero. I realise now that she was my heroin. I miss the little things; the way she used to end every phone call by saying 'stay happy,' the way she would always ask me if she had chocolate on her lips and then I would kiss her. I miss her telling me about her day and complaining about my taste in music. I miss the way she smells, the perfume she wore. Most of all I miss her smile. The way she used to look at me; the great moments in our relationship when things were perfect.'

'Are you going to be okay?' James offered me a tissue and put his hand on my shoulder. 'Things happen for a reason Vinny.'

Since James and I talked I felt more comfortable in London. I still missed Dublin but I was phoning Emily every day and we talked more now than we did when I was there. I rang my parents a lot more and my mother gave me lots of advice. My father offered me financial support but I managed to support myself.

I thought about Claire and wrote her a letter every week. I never sent any of them but kept them under my bed. The laptop that I was given for my birthday was not expensive but perfect for me. I began to type what I had written and changed a few things with the story line. I kept my idea of a pre heaven and called it Eden. I kept on referring to sections in both the Old and New Testaments.

Because I had a laptop, I found that I was typing everywhere. On quiet nights at the restaurant, I would bring my laptop downstairs and start typing in-between taking orders. I liked getting out the house and the laptop gave me a chance to find new surroundings where I could type.

Late September and Little Italy had become even quieter again. There were fewer tourists and it started getting colder so more people were staying at home. One night it was only Jake the chef and me on shift, which meant that we got over excited when we saw a customer. We closed early and I stayed in the restaurant to finish typing up what I had already written.

Typing the pages took longer than I originally thought. I was redrafting as I was retyping which lengthened the process considerably. I did not realise it would take so much out of me to write a book. Writing a book is almost an impossible task, it is not actually writing that is hard, if you have a good idea, it can be quite easy to write but it is the distractions that make you spend an entire night writing less than a page. I reluctantly removed the solitaire card game from my computer and returned to work.

At around half past twelve I woke to a deafening knock at the restaurant door. I opened my eyes and saw Kate standing at the doorway, crying. The torrential rain outside had drenched her. I jumped from my chair and unlocked the door. As I unlocked the door, she flung her arms around me.

'Oh Vinny,' she cried, 'the bastard hit me!'

'Are you okay?' I asked trying to wake myself up,

'I'm fine, it's just…' and she continued to cry. For about ten minutes, she blubbered and I, like any other man in my position just listened. I picked out certain words through the screeching, which allowed me to follow her situation. I remembered what James said about giving advice and considered it with my response.

‘Would you like some water?’ I asked, she nodded and I poured her a glass of water.

‘I can’t believe he hit me. I used to think women who went out with blokes that hit them were idiots,’

‘What happened?’ I asked,

‘We were talking about moving to a bigger place and the subject of money came up. We talked about our jobs and as a joke; I asked him if he was sleeping with his manageress. He became defensive and accused me of cheating on him. We both brought up things we argued about in the past. He eventually lost his temper and he hit me,’ she seemed both angry and scared at the same time.

‘Kate, it’s okay. You did the right thing by coming here. Are you injured?’

‘No, not badly; it’s just shock more than anything. I’m glad I have you as a friend,’

‘No problem. That’s what I’m here for,’ she laughed at this and I told her some awful jokes to make her smile. We spent a couple of hours talking about relationships and love.

‘Love is a con,’ she announced,

‘You can’t really believe that,’ I argued,

'Sure,' she smiled at me, 'love is something that is over hyped and makes you feel like crap when it all goes wrong,'

'It doesn't always go wrong,' I thought about my current situation, 'take my parents for example, they've been together since what seems to be the beginning of time and they seem happy,'

'Things have changed though; people are becoming less dependant on each other,'

'I haven't, I'm still the same female-dependant male that I always was,'

'You're not woman-dependent at the moment,'

'Yeah, but I'm suffering because of it. My hair is messy and out of control, I still have that unpleasant crust in my eyes and I can't cook. I will always be woman-dependant but now I'm just in between women,'

'You wish,' as she said this she laughed. I finally got the joke and laughed too.

'I'm tired, do you think it'll be okay to spend the night here?'

'Yeah, James won't mind. I'll sleep on the sofa, take my bed,'

'I don't mind sleeping on the sofa,'

'I insist,' and as I finished speaking, she kissed me. It was more than a kiss; we shared a moment, for a second I could not breathe. She left the room and I exhaled and opened my eyes. A moment of disbelief questioned what just happened.

The next day I awoke on the sofa. James was in the kitchen,

'Morning!' said James, 'did I wake you?'

'Nah, I'm okay' I stretched my arms and closed my eyes,

'What's Kate doing in your bed?'

'Um… She had to sleep here last night,' I mumbled, 'long story,'

'No problem,' he replied, 'I'm just going to sort a few things out, I'll be back at around twelve,'

'Okay,' I muttered half asleep. I reached over to the remote for the stereo and my Matchbox Twenty album was already in the machine. I let the soft vocals of Rob Thomas put me back to sleep.

What seemed to be a few minutes later, Kate came and perched on the sofa.

'Hi,' she said in a soft voice, I pretended to stay asleep and she kissed me.

'Hi,' I looked up at her and she looked like an angel. Her eyes seemed so big.

'I have to go. You can have your bed back,' she whispered.

'Where are you going?'

'I have to go and see my mother,'

'Okay,' I nodded off and returned to my mid morning dreamlike state. I eventually summoned the energy to go back to my own bed and buried myself in the duvet. I returned to my tranquil slumber.

I awoke in a good mood and made myself a nice big fried breakfast. I watched cartoons for most of the afternoon and finally sat down to write another chapter. I began to think about religion more than I used to. I am not religious and I believe that most organised religion is a direct cause of many of the major wars.

However, religion is a human commodity that gives us comfort and guidance. My personal belief is that all the main religious texts were written by man and should be observed as a metaphor rather than genuine events that occurred in history.

Nonetheless, I wanted to tackle a subject that many people could not fathom. Who or what created God? Why are we here? Who are we?

I liked the idea of this prequel because it gives insight into questions that we should be asking. The only problem I could conceive now is that I did not want to be misunderstood. I am a writer who has created a fictional story set before time. I am not going to explain the existence of life but instead question it.

I wrote more that day but most of it resulted in deletion. I had to be very careful not to offend or undermine a culture. I did however visualise how I wanted the young God to appear. I gave my central character more depth and even at some points, human endeavour.

I was thinking more now than ever before and I was beginning to accept my new life. At first, it seemed like a temporary solution. Claire would ring me and I would go home. Things would eventually go back to normal. I could comprehend the possibility of that not happening and found solace in the realisation of that truth. I live in London.

I called Emily and explained to her that the possibility of me not returning was high. For the first time in a while, I was home sick. I missed my old house, I missed Emily and most of all I missed Claire. I had accepted the fact that this was my life now and it was time to move on.

october

The winds of Eden became heavier on that glorious day. My elder brother, Lucifer, meditated in his private kingdom while I admired his strength and convictions. Our father favoured me most, which angered him but he never exposed his rage. We worshiped our father and remained his subjects.

Kate was living with her mother temporarily, which meant that she cut down on her shifts. I realised at this time that I actually hated being a waiter. The reason I loved the job initially was that I was working with Kate; being around her concealed the repetitive and tedious elements of the job.

The truth of the matter is simple. I am a bad waiter. I am someone who had spent the majority of their life working with numbers and computers. I had gained some common sense but I cannot do a job like this forever. James is a great person to work for but I was getting unbelievably bored.

I was thinking of finding a job in the city. Do what I was doing before but in London instead. I wanted to finish the book first and I enjoy living with James and Kelly. I thought about what I sought after in life. I felt depressed but I could not figure out why. I think that everyone goes through a short period of melancholy, whether they're happy or not. I initially put it down to the weather but I knew subconsciously that it was more than that.

I spent the day with my laptop in the restaurant. I was not working that day but I felt I needed to be in an environment with people around me. I pretended that I was a customer and drank numerous cups of coffee. James would occasionally sit with me but for the most part, I squandered the time staring at a blank screen. I was worried about how critics would assassinate my use of diction. The element of being a writer is that you have to live up to expectations of higher diction and complex sentence structures.

The restaurant was quiet that evening and I found that I spend most of my time daydreaming. I knew that my accommodation was temporary and I did not want to outstay my welcome. I had mentioned moving out to James but every time I said something, he would insist that I stayed. I wanted to have my own place again and regain that feeling of independence.

I bought the Guardian and looked for jobs in the city. I remembered the job I used to do and how it took over my life. I recollect the sleepless nights worrying about the future of the company. I recall going on Saturdays and working late almost every night. But most of all, I remember the people I used to work with, the pretentious and self serving individuals who committed themselves to a company so they could compete with who has the better lifestyle.

I liked my old dwelling but I no longer miss it. I have found solace in my writing and it makes me far more content than my widescreen television. Even if I am not published, I will be satisfied with the knowledge that I have produced something creative. My book is the epicentre of my life and is the result of a realised ambition.

I observe the people that come into the restaurant and incorporate them into my characters. People are fascinating; I watch how people act when they encounter other people. A young man comes in and spends an hour watching Cristina work. He eats and I can see him trying to gain the courage to ask her out but he never does it.

On some days, we have a group of executives that come in after work and have their staff meeting over dinner. Each of them pretends to be something their not. The drink expensive wine and talk about art and books but never talk on a personal level.

I find that I sometimes think about the decisions I have made in life and question how things would be if I could go back and make a different decision. I remind myself on how lucky I am to have the things I have but still feel envious of people that have more than I do. I want to be thinner and more intelligent. I want to have perfect cheekbones and manageable hair. I want to travel to exotic islands and eat at the finest restaurants but I know deep down that this does not make you a better person.

A year ago, I knew where I would be in five years time. Now I have no idea where my life will lead. I find it amusing how people change. As humans, we evolve mentally as well as physically. I have never been emotionally as strong as I am now. Darwin's theory of evolution extends to the psychological aspect of existence. My father always said that whatever does not kill you will make you stronger.

Kate has moved in with her mother, which means it takes her almost an hour to get to work and she does not have to pay rent. She has reduced her hours because of this. Saturday however, she was at work and I insisted that I work that shift too. James took Kelly out for their anniversary and left me in charge. We were very quiet that evening and so Kate and I spent most of the evening sitting at the bar and talking.

For some reason the few customers that we did have, were couples. Kate and I took turns to serve them. At nine o'clock, James phoned to inform me that they were not coming home that evening and booked themselves into a posh hotel. I told him not to worry about a thing and that I would close up. I asked Kate if she would help me to close up,

'I can't' she replied, 'the last bus to my mother's house is at eleven'

'Stay the night' I blurted this out without thinking. Surely, she would not even consider it. 'I mean, if you can then…' she looked at me and I had absolutely no idea what she was thinking, 'I'll sleep on the sofa, like last time'

'Okay' she said,

'Great! I mean... um...' I had no idea what to say to her.

'I'm just going to give my mother a quick call.'

'No problem,' I smiled and cheerfully served another couple that entered the restaurant. We concentrated on the customers until about eleven o'clock and then we became quiet again.

'I'm glad I'm not going home,' Kate said as we were sitting by the bar,

'Really?' I became intrigued.

'Yeah, I hate living with my mum, she drives me crazy.'

'Oh, what are you going to do?'

'I'm going to start looking for a place' she replied. As she said this, I thought about us living together and decided to suggest it.

'Well, how about you and I... y'know'

'What? Live together? I don't know Vinny; it doesn't sound like a good idea.'

‘What’s not a good idea? We both need to find a place and there is no way either of us can afford to live on our own. It makes sense,’

‘What if things go wrong?’

‘Well, it’s better than living with your mother and if things turn sour then I’ll move out.’

‘Okay, I’ll think about it.’

‘Great,’ I like the idea of living with Kate. Kate checked on some customers and I started cleaning the bar. Mark, the chef, had finished cleaning the kitchen. I booked him a taxi and he left. Mark never really talked to anyone at work but we seemed to get on well enough. At midnight, Kate and I decided we were hungry so we raided the fridge and Kate opened a bottle of wine. We had a glass each but neither of us wanted to get drunk.

I told her that I was thinking about not finishing the novel and this surprised her. She asked me why I first came to London, I told her how Claire had left me and I came to realise my dream of being a novelist. She reminded me of my ambition and the reason I was here. I was feeling dejected for the best part of the week but being with her then made me forget that I was me. She made me feel contented.

'I love you' I said. She looked at me for a minute and said nothing, 'I love you Kate, and not in a misplaced affection way. I've been trying to tell you this for so long and I need you to know how I feel. I have no choice but to tell you, even if it ruins our friendship. I can't live without looking into your eyes or wanting to hold you. I have never felt like this, only people in illusionary romantic films feel like this but my words cannot express my feelings towards you. I can't let another day go by without displaying my affections for you. I know if I ever meet someone else who is half of what you are and what you mean to me, I'll be happy. Kate…' and with a tear rolling down her face, she leaned over and kissed me.

She let her forehead rest on mine. I stared deeply into her eyes. It was like being in the forest in my book. She was my Eden, and I was lost in her eyes.

'I love you too Vinny' she whispered. We went upstairs; I turned the CD player on and she turned the lights down. We both rushed into the middle of the room and kissed like fifteen-year-olds at a school disco. I ran my fingers through her soft brown hair. She started to unbutton my shirt and pulled me into the bedroom. We slowly undressed each other but we never stopped that kiss. That night I reached my Shangri-La.

The next morning we woke to the sound of James and Kelly returning. James called from the living room,

'Vinny, are you okay?'

'Yeah, yeah,' I yelled back. Kate hid under the covers as he entered into the room.

'Hey buddy, still asleep?' James asked

'Yeah, I was just about to get up… um… how was your evening?' I asked, he could tell I was nervous about something,

'Good, we had fun,' James noticed a bra on the floor and he picked it up, 'Vinny, is there something you want to tell me?' I laughed as he said this and he pulled my covers back slightly revealing Kate. James stood there stunned,

'Kelly!' he shouted towards the door, 'look at what Vinny did!' Kate threw a pillow at James, which he caught. Kelly walked into the room and saw Kate and me in bed together. She automatically burst into laughter and grabbed James's arm.

'Leave them alone,' Kelly said while pulling James out of the room. Kate and I looked at each other and began to laugh. We began to kiss again and we heard laughter from the living room. Kate and I got dressed and faced the inquisition in the kitchen. James made some lunch and both Kelly and James tried not to say anything.

'So, how was it?' James asked with a big grin on his face. Kelly slapped him on the back of his head.

'I think you make a nice couple,' said Kelly while she gave James a stern look. We ate lunch and Kate returned to her mother's house. I confessed the whole story, minus precious details, to James and Kelly that evening. I knew if I said nothing, they would both make my life hell.

Kate and I spent the next two weeks relishing in our honeymoon period. We went to the theatre and she even took me ice-skating. We started looking at apartments near the restaurant.

In the space of that initial two weeks, we accomplished more in our relationship than most people do in a year. Things between us were moving very quickly and neither of us seemed too bothered about it. She talked to Connor and told him that she would never forgive him. After her last visit to see him, neither of us ever heard from him again.

We found a nice little flat near the restaurant. It seemed a little early to move in together but it seemed right. The apartment was on the third floor and was quite small. Our new home was nothing special and it was expensive but we did not care; we were happy being together. The letting agent showed us around in less than five minutes and after careful consideration, we decided to take it.

Kate moved her things in first I brought my few possessions over the following day. James put me on the payroll and I received a proper wage. I found it easier to write now I had my own place. I felt more comfortable because I was in my own environment. Kate bought a few pictures that she hung on the wall and I bought a second hand sofa where I could nap. It seemed a tad early to move in together but we both needed somewhere to live but it made more sense, than not, to share a place. It just happened that we were in love with each other.

The two weeks from when Kate and I officially became a couple and moved in together, were the most hectic but enjoyable two weeks of my life. When Claire and I first lived together we argued after the first two days but with Kate, it is impossible to argue. She is the most rational person I have had the privilege to know and because of this, we always seemed to find common ground.

The weather began to get colder and we would spend the nights we had off work, curling up on the sofa and watching television. I tried not to compare living with Kate and living with Claire but sometimes, I did it without even realising. I knew that things between Kate and I would not always be a bed of roses but I felt a stronger connection with Kate. I had only known Kate for a few months but part of me felt like I had known her for years. Things between Kate and I were destined and for the first time in my life I actually believed in fate.

I had a lengthy telephone conversation with Emily on a frosty Thursday evening at the end of the month. Emily and I talked on almost a daily basis and we always had something to talk about however tedious. Emily had been ringing me on my mobile phone because I did not have a landline.

Later that evening, Kate was working at the restaurant and I decided to spend the evening writing. On that fateful evening, my phone rang. It was the number that Emily usually calls me from but it was too late in the evening to be Emily. Intrigued, I answered the call.

'Hello?'

'Hi Vinny, it's me,' came a reminiscent sombre voice,

'Claire?'

'Yeah,' she replied,

'How are you?' I asked. I did not know what to say,

'I'm good, I just…' she paused, 'I just wanted to hear your voice,'

'Oh,' I replied. Hearing her voice was very peculiar,

'Vinny I'm sorry. I did not mean to hurt you. I made a mistake.' I could hear her crying, 'I still love you.'

'Claire, I'm sorry but this is too much,' I was angry but part of me still loved her. 'Claire, I'm sorry but I can't do this,' and I put the phone down. I sat in disbelief at what had just happened. I rang James and told him what happened. He came over to see me because I knew Kate would be at the restaurant. I told him what had just occurred and he listened to what I had to say. I had to choose between Claire and Kate. Technically, I was still married to Claire but I was living with Kate.

On the one hand, I had a wife and a daughter and on the other hand, I was in love and on the verge of accomplishing an ambition. I was trapped in a life changing decision and James tried to comfort me. He tried to understand what I was going through. Most people have been in the situation where they have to choose a path and I knew then that if I made the wrong decision, I would suffer the consequences.

I did not sleep that night. Kate knew there was something wrong but she did not say anything. I know that with Claire, I am walking down a path I have trodden before. I was still angry with Claire and I knew if I returned to Dublin, I would be reminded of what she did to me. I missed Emily like crazy but that was not enough. I know that couples should not stay together for the children and Emily would be better off if we were separated. Subsequently, I had only known Kate for about seven months.

When did life become so complicated? I am faced here with the hardest decision I have ever had to make and I have no idea what to do. I love my life in London. Will I still love it when it becomes permanent? What if I choose Kate and she leaves me? What if I return to Claire and she leaves me again? I needed time to think and assess the situation.

november

The Grounds of Eden began to rumble as my brother's rage cast a shadow over the Holy Kingdom. Deity verses deity in the midst of existence. I never knew who struck first but watched in fear. After the tempest of emotions, my brother Lucifer consequently fell to his feet. My Father banished his spirit into the ground leaving only his memory in my mind. The Holy Spirit decreed that a deity might only have one son from this day forth so such occasion would never occur. My Father appointed me the new ruler of heaven while he would be the eternal protector of Eden.

My mind was telling me to stay with Claire because of Emily but my heart was telling me to stay with Kate. I knew I could not make this decision lightly and so I told Kate the situation and she stormed out of the house. I could not expect anything less. I had the opportunity to go back to things the way they were. I had to decide on something soon or I would lose them both.

I bought some cigarettes and came home. I wanted to get drunk. I knew Kate had half a bottle of vodka in the kitchen somewhere. I rummaged through the cupboards and my rampage ended in disappointment. I collapsed on the kitchen floor, half in rage and the other in self-loathing. I stared at the white ceiling and contemplated my situation.

Suddenly there was a knock at the door. I thought it was Kate. She had come back to me and I could tell her that I loved her and things would go back to how they were. I opened the door and Claire stood there looking at me. She put on a fake smile when she saw me and I froze. I could not move from the bombshell that was staring at me on my doorstep.

'Come in' I said after a few seconds, my eyes remaining fully open,

'Thanks' she said in her soft Irish accent. She walked into the living room and stood in the middle of it.

'What are you doing here?' I asked.

'I've come to get my husband back,'

'Where's Emily?'

'She's with my mother,' she looked down for a minute and said, 'I'm sorry,'

'You know that's the first time you've apologised to me.'

'I know, I love you.'

'Stop. You've put me though hell in the last year, why should I listen to what you have to say?'

'I know you're angry with me but this was inevitable. I didn't know you would move to London,' she sounded almost patronising when she said this,

'Don't blame me for what happened. You left me. YOU LEFT ME!' I could feel the rage overcome my body as I began to tense every muscle I had.

'Vinny, please, I made a mistake. What about Emily? You don't want her to grow up without a father, do you?'

'Claire, please don't do this to me. I'm happy and in love. Don't ruin this for me,'

'I love you. You have a family. I've talked to the people at your old job and they're willing to negotiate. Things can go back to how they were,' I felt myself drawing to her. Each tear she shed weakened my senses and my inner rage began to desist. I drew closer to her and kissed her. A million thoughts were running through my head and suddenly one stood out. I pulled away from our kiss,

'No,'

'Honey? What?'

'No, I'm not letting you do this to me again,'

'Vinny please!'

'No Claire. You chose him. For the past year I have only remembered the good times but things between us were dead a long time ago, I can't do this anymore.' We both had tears in our eyes.

'I'm sorry. Come back, if not for me then your daughter,'

'I'm not staying with you for Emily's sake. I love my daughter and would give anything to make her happy but in the long term it will make things harder,'

'You bastard!' she screamed.

'You left me Claire, for him. If things had worked out between you two, then you would not be feeling like this. You chose him. I'm sorry.'

'I have to go' she whispered, she got her things and headed towards the door.

‘Claire, I meant what I said about Emily, you can’t deny me seeing my daughter,’ as I said this she stopped and paused. She looked around in anger and screamed,

‘You bastard! You want your new girlfriend and to see your daughter?’

‘I had no choice, you left me Claire. I had to find a new life, you made me,’

‘I’ll send the divorce papers through the post,’ she announced and ran out of the building in tears.

I returned to the sofa and sat. My mind was trying to comprehend the situation I had just experienced. Divorced at the age of twenty-seven. I did not know what to do but continue to cry. I decided to ring my mother and find solace in her. We spent an hour talking and she gave me good rational advice. Then my father asked to speak to me and I explained the whole situation. I will always remember his words.

‘Are you an Idiot? Go after Kate before she leaves you too,’ and then my father hung up. I knew Kate would be at her mother’s house. I quickly tried to brush my hair but gave up after a few seconds and put on my shoes. I grabbed my coat and ran through the heavy November rain. After I realised the underground would take too long, I ran to a vacant taxi. I paid the taxi driver extra to break the speed limit and arrived at her mother's house late that evening.

I knocked on the door but there was no answer. I jumped over the back gate and tried to see which room belonged to Kate. There was only one light on and I assumed it would be hers. I threw small stones gently at the second floor window. Eventually she looked out the window.

'Kate! I'm sorry, I love you!'

'What about her Vinny? What about your wife?'

'It's over between us, it has been for almost a year, she just forgot,'

'Vinny, I'm not sure,'

'I love you. I cannot imagine my life without you. I love the way you speak and the way you walk. I love everything about you. I never thought love really existed and people just settle with the people they love at the time they want to commit but you changed that, you. I realise now that love does exist and I truly love you. You are the epitome of everything I look for in a woman. You fill that empty hole in my stomach. I love you, Kate.' The heavy rain hid my tears.

'Wait there!' she called from the window,

'What?!' I replied and then her bedroom light turned off. I looked at the ground and realised that I was completely soaked. Then a light appeared in the dining room. She stood in a white night-gown and opened the patio doors. I walked towards her and she ran towards me. We embraced.

'Kate, I'm sorry, I love you…' I began to stutter from the cold and she silenced me,

'Stop talking, you talk too much,' and she kissed me. We continued to kiss and never stopped kissing.

One of the reasons I stayed with Kate is because she inspired me to write. I would watch her sleep and be inspired. On average, I wrote over two thousand words a day when I was with Kate.

Things were better than before. We rented out lots of Al Pacino films and I sat through Pretty Woman and actually enjoyed it but I never admitted this to Kate. We became one of those couples that did everything and for the first time in my life, I felt content.

One frosty morning Kate woke before I did. She went into the kitchen to make tea and found a letter in the post. It had been redirected from the restaurant to our flat. Half asleep, I asked Kate to open it. It was a letter from a major bank confirming an interview and practically offering me a job.

'When did you apply for this?' Kate asked.

'A while ago, I think,' I murmured with my eyes closed and comfortably cased in my duvet.

'I thought you were going to finish the book?'

'I am, I just thought at the time that it would be prudent to get a high paid job,'

'I thought you hated being an accountant,'

'Financial advisor, and yes I hated it. I spent all my time working,'

'Are you going to the interview?'

'I don't know,'

'Vinny,' Kate pulled me over, 'I don't want you to take this job, my mother always told me to follow your dreams. Will you finish the book?'

'Yeah,'

'Promise me,'

'I'll finish the book, why are you upset by this?' I asked,

'I just don't want you to give up on your dreams,'

'Okay, I promise,' and with that she disappeared into the kitchen. I returned to my mid morning nap.

That evening I thought about what Kate had said. I remember Claire always pushing me to get a promotion then complaining because I was always at the office working. Kate understood that she could have either the money or me. And she chose to have me around. Kate would rather I be happy than eat at fancy restaurants every week or have the perfect house. I had told her about my last job and the people that I used to work with. I told her about the late nights and how my job contributed to the break up of my marriage with Claire.

Kate had dated a workaholic before and we both realised that that is not what we wanted. I knew I had to finish the book and that was my main priority. I re-read the beginning of the Old Testament and realised the best way to end my book is by using the beginning of Genesis.

I wanted to concentrate on the relationship between fathers and their sons rather than concentrate wholly on the religious aspect. I was nearing the end of the hundred thousand words that I now set myself. Like Milton, I split my book into sub books to give it a genuine ambience. I sectioned it into four books.

Rather than write in an archaic text, I wrote it like a modern day novel but still maintained the sense of an epic saga. I used events in both the Old Testament and the New Testament to create prophecies narrated by the Holy Spirit. I even managed to surpass my own expectations. I was now beginning to write the final book and continued the same atmosphere throughout. I tried no to be cliché but on some levels, that would be impossible.

The idea of a fight between the Holy Spirit and Lucifer would be spectacular but the idea of God showing human emotions and recreating an angel in his brother's likeness would be a good ending. I knew how I wanted to end it but I still found that something was missing. I wanted to add prophecies about our world and really cause some disparagement from the extreme religious groups and the critics.

Part of me just wanted to finish the book and get it over and done with. We all do things that we regret later but after we have accomplished our goals we recollect with contented joy at the experience, we underwent. The only person I let read the novel was Kate but she said she would never give me any constructive criticism until I had finished the book.

I thought about the thousands upon thousands of writers in the world and how, unless I won the Pulitzer, would never accomplish fame. However, fame was never an issue; the book is a reward in itself. I did however want to be published. If I could inspire one person then my ambitions would be complete.

Kate had told James about the job so when I arrived to work that day, James approached me.

'Kate tells me you got offered an office job, why didn't you take it?'

'Kate told you that?' I asked,

'Vinny, you're my favourite waiter but I don't want you to waste your life doing this,'

'Firstly, I'm your only waiter and secondly, I have been down that path before. Jobs like this come and go but how often do you fall in love and realise an ambition?'

'You're right Vinny,' James smiled, 'I'm glad you came to London. You've become a good friend. That's why I wanted to ask you something,'

'Anything'

'Will you be my best man at my wedding?'

'I'm honoured. I would be privileged.'

'Thanks Vinny, I'm going to ask Kelly on Christmas Day.'

'That's great James,' I gave him a hug, which was strange because I was not used to hugging James. I told him that I would go ring shopping with him. I saw the difference now, between Sean and James. I would always like to think of them as brothers.

We were becoming increasingly busy in the restaurant and I found that I had become a good waiter. When Kate and I worked together, we would always slip into the kitchen, kiss until James catches us, and tell us to get back to work. I loved working at Little Italy even though I was being paid less than when I was working at university. I came to the realisation that money was no longer important. I did not want a big television with a DVD or a giant stereo in my living room.

That evening I rang Emily and we talked about how my situation has become permanent. I told her that I would come, visit her on Boxing Day, and stay for a few days. I promised that I would come and see her and she could come and see me in the holidays.

I told Emily to listen to her mother and be a good girl while she was staying at her grandmother's house. We talked about the future and she told me she wanted to be a writer when she grew up. We talked about how Aunt Michelle was having a baby soon and I asked her what she wanted for Christmas.

After we talked for an hour, I told her I loved her. I promised that I would never stop being her father and would ring her every other day. A promise I have never broken.

december

On that day, I created the Heavens. I constructed a holy army of Angels of which I appointed a leader. Lucifer, the first and most prominent arc angel, created in the likeness of my own dear brother. My heaven is created and from here, our story begins.

I screamed as I wrote the last word of my book. My hands were in the air and I felt like a god. I could not describe the feeling. I was literally jumping. I, Vinny Thomas, had written a book! I have become a novelist. I am now a writer. I knew I had to find a publisher and go through legal processes to get the novel copyrighted.

I had to reread through it to make sure I did not make any silly mistakes. I woke Kate to tell her I had finished but she did not seem too enthusiastic at four in the morning. I decided to get some sleep and lay marvelling at my own accomplishment. I decided to end the book when God had finished creating the heavens.

I actually liked my own book. I know that most authors tend to develop a hatred for their work but I actually liked how the book was formed. I knew that the fact that I had no previous literary endeavours of any merit would mean that it would be impossible for me to be published but being published was not a main concern of mine. I was simply ecstatic that I had actually finished the book.

I had asked James previously if I could borrow his printer and the following day I bought paper and a print cartridge. The following day I woke James at ten o'clock in the morning with laptop in hand and ready to print. While the document was printing, I let James read it. He read the first twenty pages and told me he would read the rest later. I made him breakfast and we talked about the book.

James returned to bed while I explored the Internet for publishers. I had a wide library of books with the addresses of publishers printed on the copyright pages. I made a list of about twenty publishers who may have an interest in publishing my book. I found a company that would develop various transcripts of the book and a law company that would copyright it for me.

Two hours later I had a hard copy of the book in my hands. It was over two hundred pages on A4 and contained over two hundred thousand words. I read extracts and forgot that I wrote them. I realised then that someone was actually going to read it and decide to either recommend it or warn others not to read it.

I began to think about the cover and decided I wanted it to be antiquated and make it look like a very old copy of the bible. The first page had only the title, 'The Holy Bible: A Prequel.'

I left the dedication page open because I still had not decided to whom it was that I would bestow that honour. Originally, the book was going to be dedicated to Claire when I thought the possibility of us becoming a couple again was conceivable.

The dedication gave me great insight on how I prioritise the people in my life. James and Kelly have been like family for me in the last eight months and it is because of Kate that I finished the book. Sean has been a good friend and has allowed me to discuss ideas with him. All these people would be in the dedication.

I began to think about Claire. Her decision to leave me in the first place initiated the fact that I would consider writing at all. I knew that Claire and her infatuation with her religion made me rebel against her in most of our arguments. Claire initially inspired me with the story line after a heated discussion about organised religion and the fact that when I was with her, all I would ever be was a financial advisor.

When Claire and I ended our relationship, it hurt me. I realise now that Claire will always be a part of my life and I would never forget her. In a perfect world, we would still be together and this year would not have even happened. I will always love Claire and I know deep down, she will always love me.

Things change and people change. From that fateful day almost a year ago, I stopped planning my life. I might even meet someone else but I know that there is no point thinking about those things. It is time for me to live for now and stop thinking about the future.

I came to the realisation that I had to dedicate the book to someone more permanent. I realised then the most important person in my life is Emily. Emily is the epicentre of my world as she will always be my daughter. She could move to the ends of the earth but will always be my daughter.

I wanted to dedicate the book to Kate because some part of me knew that even if I never saw her again, I would always be indebted to her for allowing me to fall in love for the second time. The first page of the novel read, 'To Emily and Kate, who I will always love,'

I put everyone that had inspired me in the last year down in the acknowledgements beginning with Kate. I mentioned my parents, Sean and Michelle. I thanked James and Kelly while mentioning Little Italy. James thought it would be a good advertisement.

I wanted to mention Claire in the acknowledgements because she was a significant part of my life. 'And finally to Claire, my first love who inspired me to write the book,' this was my closure. I printed out another copy that I wrapped in brown paper ready to take to my solicitor. I took the original copy and returned home.

I opened the front door and saw Kate reading the newspaper in the kitchen. She saw me and smiled. I walked up to her and without saying a word, I gave her the copy.

'I thought you'd finished the book in my dream' she said as she took the pages from me. 'Congratulations honey, I'm proud of you.' She opened the first page and saw her name. She embraced me and said, 'thank you,'

'I love you Kate. I always will. You made this happen for me,' we remained in each other's arms both with tears in our eyes. She began to read it while I made some tea. Kate read the whole thing in two days and told me it was the best book she had ever read. I appreciated that she is biased in her opinion but felt uplifted at the fact that she enjoyed it and was the first person to read it from cover to cover. She understood that I had to mention Claire and did not feel threatened or angry by this.

A week before Christmas I got a call from Sean, 'Vinny!' came a muffled voice from the receiver,

'Sean, are you okay?'

'Yeah, I'm just… hospital…' he was out of breath and sounded as if he was in shock,

'Sean, what's happened?'

'I… I… I'm a dad,'

'Oh my God! Congratulations buddy! Is Michelle okay?'

'Yeah, we have a beautiful baby boy.' I've never heard Sean like this, he is usually more reserved, 'we've called him Vincent,' and then I went silent. All I could think about was this poor child that was given the name Vincent and part of me felt gratified at the fact that Sean did this for me.

'Thank you Sean. You're going to make a good father.'

'My God! Vinny this is amazing; I've never felt like this before,'

'Have you rung James yet?'

'Yeah, I rang James and my parents. I'm going to ring everyone else later. Listen, I'll ring you tomorrow when it has all sunk in,'

'No problem,' and with that the conversation ended. I sat in amazement, then went upstairs to Kate, and told her the good news. The idea of Sean being a father made me realise that we are grown-ups. Sean, the guy who woke up wearing a wedding dress on the day of his wedding, is now a father.

This inspired me to ring my parents and I told them how much I loved them. I thought about how parents are role models for their children and it was because of my parents that I am happy now.

I rang James and we talked about the fact that Sean was a father and he made jokes about the poor boy's name. We laughed at the fact that James was an uncle and then he reminded me that to Sean and himself, I am also an uncle.

Sean rang me that evening and he divulged in the details of the birth. Sean described the birth of his son like an awakening and we discussed the fact that we have all become adults and inevitably turned into our parents. Sean becoming a parent was signified a change in all of us. The birth of young Vincent made us reflect on what has happened and re-evaluate our lives.

After my lengthy conversation with Sean, I took a moment to be nostalgic. I thought about my life at the beginning of the year and what I had achieved after all that I have endured and what events I have yet to face.

I thought about Emily and young Vincent, which made me realise that they too will face the same rights of passage. I knew what I wanted to do with my life now and I was fortunate to know whom I wanted to spend it with.

This morning was brighter than the other mornings. It was not snowing outside but there was a thin layer of frost over most things. I snuggled up in the duvet and saw Kate lying adjacent to me. I ran my fingers through her soft brown hair and stared at the ceiling. I decided to get up and make her breakfast in bed.

In the kitchen, I grilled some bacon and cut some soft white rolls. I lightly cascaded the brown sauce over the bacon and put the bacon rolls on a plate. I made some tea and put it all on a tray with a single stem rose. I brought it into the room and gently woke Kate. She opened her big brown eyes and smiled at me.

'Merry Christmas honey,' she uttered in a daze,

'Merry Christmas Katie,' and I gave her a kiss. I presented her with breakfast and we sat in bed watching cartoons and eating. After breakfast, we exchanged presents. She got me a pen with 'To Vinny. I love you. Kate' engraved onto the side. I gave her a small wrapped box. She opened the box and inside she found an assortment of artist's tools and a note. The note read, 'go into the living room,' she quickly got out of bed and rushed into the lounge where she saw an easel. Taped to the easel were her tuition fees for the art course in Islington she wanted to do and aeroplane tickets to Ireland for the Boxing Day weekend. It would be a weekend away because she always wanted to see where I had been living before I moved to London. I told her we could stay with Sean and I could visit Emily. She gave me a hug and we thanked each other.

I rang Emily and wished her a merry Christmas. I told her that I would be in Ireland tomorrow and that she could come and visit me on Boxing Day. Emily told me that Claire spent a night at Rob's house after she got back from London but I had to keep it a secret. She told me she got lots of boring toys and clothes from Father Christmas. I told her that I would change that when I saw her. I asked her if she had seen the new baby and she told me it looked like Sean but smaller. I told her I loved her and I would see her the following evening.

After a couple of hours in bed watching television we finally showered, dressed, and arrived at Little Italy for Christmas dinner. James was wearing an awful florescent blue jumper that I assume was a Christmas present... As we entered, we were greeted with hugs and well wishes. Kate presented Kelly with a bottle of champagne and James beckoned me into the kitchen.

He signalled to me by putting a finger over his lips then exhibiting the most beautiful wedding ring in a velvet box. I smiled and gave him the thumbs up. We talked about the future while I watched him cook enough food to feed a large Italian family. James is renown for his culinary skills. Kate and Kelly talked about the presents they got and laughed about the jumper that James received from his mother.

Kelly opened a bottle of wine and we sat around the large round table to eat. James carved and we ate until we could eat no more. We sat around talking about how the same programs are repeated on television and then suddenly James asks for our attention. He gets onto one knee and proposes.

'Kelly, I know we've never talked about this before but I now know I want to spend the rest of my life with you. Would you please do me the honour of marrying me?'

'Yes! Of course, I love you,' she said instantly. They both stood and kissed. Kate and I applauded and made whooping sounds. Kate and I looked at each other, she whispered into my ear,

'My heaven is created and from here our story begins.'

acknowledgements

I would like to thank the following,

Sarah Campbell, Yuri Doric, Cindy Young and the good people at Trafford for their support and encouragement.

Clare Coleridge for the cover.

For support and encouragement, I would like to thank Satish Sedani, Bina Sedani, Shaun Sedani, Bee Kaplan, Richard Adams, Steven Newman, Steve and Jackie Stopani, Adam Brighton, Benjamin Timberley, Richard Giddings, Maggie Holman, Jake Ashton, Jenny Cheese, Claire Bruges, Kate Rhodes, Simon Featherstone, David Booy, Mary Alice McDevitt, Ryan Morris, Yann Stahmer, Matchbox Twenty, Josh Ive, Sam Protherough and Clara Machell.

I would also like to dedicate this book to my grandparents, who I miss very much.

Ricky Sedani

ISBN 155395674-5

9 781553 956747